Enchanted

Scandal

by

Tammy Sötnos

Fame's Eternal Books, LLC
United States of America

I dedicate this novel to:

Lieutenant Colonel John Thomas Peterson,
my inspiration.

Tammy Sötnos

ACKNOWLEDGMENTS

I would like to thank the following individuals for their invaluable input:
Harlequinn novelist, Lauri Robinson; and award-winning playwright/author, Elizabeth Thomas.

My proofreaders:
Richard Gensch, Cheryl Lund, Shawna Carver, and Allison Fuller.

Those providing insight during the early stages of this novel:
Lieutenant Colonel John Thomas Peterson, Jobie Guzman, Kathy Glover, and Sandy Millar.

In addition, I would like to thank Andrea Hamilton, Elizabeth Thomas, Richard Gensch, and Daniel Gensch **for their wonderful friendship and support during life's triumphs, trials, and tribulations.**

Tammy Sötnos

PREFACE

The premise of this book is based on my own reality in conjunction with my great great great grandmother's. Her name was Ursula Fina. She was a beautiful yet "lowly" peasant woman, who fell in love with a person of status in Austria. His name was Count Von Lippitzbach. Ursula's peasant status prevented the count from marrying her. However, their love produced my great great grandfather.....

Tammy Sötnos

FOREWORD

Enchanted Scandal is told from Samantha's perspective. However, you will notice instances when Samantha is not present yet action continues. I add these moments to make the story more fun. Therefore, if you find yourself saying, "How could Samantha know this occurred? She's not even in the room," please keep in mind that your author only added the particular scene to make the novel more enjoyable to read.

Additionally, I would like to address dialogue. I find the language of 18th century England to be wordy and at times laborious/boring. Therefore, I have chosen for my characters' dialogue to include a flavor of the actual language yet tightened with the language of today for a smoother, more comfortable read.

Blessings!

Tammy Sötnos

Chapter 1

Her sparkling eyes followed his bare, athletic derrière as he leaped out of bed and traversed the stately room of the Old Castle Inn in search of his goose quill pen. They had finished making love for the third time since reuniting only the evening before. During several hours prior to reuniting, he reconnoitered in the outskirts of the Cotswolds of England, where they resided in separate homes. The year was 1769.

"What are you looking for, Love?"

"I must pen a letter to my cousin Theodore in London. I trust he will assist me with my escape to the American Colonies."

Samantha, momentarily hurt by the thought of his leaving her, regained her composure. "Okay, Handsome." She closed her eyes and fell asleep.

At 46, his robust physique equaled that of a much younger man; while hers, at 37, revealed a voluptuously-built, lusty constitution.

Several minutes later, Samantha awoke to the feeling that someone stared at her. She opened her eyes and smiled. *John!* "What are you doing?"

"Staring at you, Beautiful." He smiled.

Samantha blushed, and held out her arms for him to come to her.

Obliging, he said, "I can only hold you a short duration. I must leave to find my messenger."

He pulled away the covers, and kissed the erect tips of each breast. His tongue entered and probed her mouth for a long, sensual while.

Finally, he gazed lovingly into her eyes. "I'll be back at dusk for our last night together...."

She hugged him tightly.

After he left, she prayed. *Thank you, dear Lord, for the magnificent time I have had with John. He has been a fantastic escape. Not only has he been kind, loving, and wonderful; he has* been *thoughtful and courageous.* Please watch over him, and keep him safe.

My life has changed so much during the past year! Samantha lay back to reflect on it:

One year ago, she had awoken to a beautiful, sunny, but frigid January day. She peeked outside the back kitchen door of her tiny cottage, and smiled at the sight of the fresh snow which made everything appear neat and tidy. Happily humming, she set the kitchen table with her pewter porringers, and prepared breakfast for her husband and children who still slept.

Suddenly, a loud noise jarred her, and everything went black. As her sight returned, her eyes bulged. *Harold must have hit me on the head...* Her husband stood holding the inflexible instrument which struck her—his favorite pewter tankard.

"A decent wife would have brought her husband a drink in bed by now!" Harold growled. "But not you! No, you busy yourself thinking *only* of yourself *as is your habit!* What must ye say for yourself?"

Still drunk from the night before—which for him had ended only an hour prior to the assault, Harold raised his tankard again and threatened, "Answer me, or ye'll get more where this is comin' from!"

Teetering back and forth, Samantha managed to steady her body by grabbing hold of the heavy, wooden kitchen table nearby.

Harold swung his arm in a failed, drunken attempt to hit her again. Before he could swing a third time, she threw down a chair in front of him and ran out the kitchen door into the snow-covered world outside—dressed only in her nightgown. She ran as fast as she could through thick snow, with no clear trail. *Lord, help me!*

Slipping and sliding, she plowed forward over hills and down ravines until she reached the edge of the town of Painswick.

Stopping in her tracks, she made eye contact with a gentleman who appeared safe. *Maybe he can help me.*

Approaching him, she whimpered, "I think I am about to faint, sir."

"Drop into my arms," he commanded.

She obeyed, and all went black.

Samantha awoke later, and found herself ensconced in a comfortable bed with soft, fluffy blankets in an elegant bedchamber lit by candlelight. Peering out of a nearby Crown glass window, she realized, *The entire day must have passed. The sky is dark as coal!*

Attempting to gain a wider perspective, she turned her head and gasped upon catching sight of the gentleman into whose arms she had fallen. He sat in a nearby chair...asleep.

She looked down at herself and beheld the beautiful nightgown she now wore. Running her hand along one of its sleeves, she marveled, *Such fine material! Nothing like the rough cloth Harold provides me.*

Her next thought disturbed her, and she voiced, "Who put this on me?"

The sound of her voice awoke the gentleman, whose visage quickly shifted from pleasant to serious.

Samantha dove under the covers and trembled.

"Don't be afraid, my lady! I promise not to hurt you. My only wish is to be of help!"

Samantha waited a moment, and then rolled down the covers to just below her eyes. *The honesty in his eyes calms me.*

She sat upright. "Who dressed me in this night gown?"

"So that is what upsets you. Do not trouble yourself, my lady. My *maidservants* assisted you. I assure you they handled you with the *utmost* of privacy."

Disconcerted still, Samantha asked, "May I have my own bed gown returned to me?"

"I shan't think you will have need of it. My servants have washed the blood from it. It is fully damp as we speak."

"Blood?" Samantha inquired. *Oh, of course...*

The word *blood* reminded Samantha of what had recently transpired—the incident which sent her fleeing into frigid weather dressed only in her nightgown. She solemnly reached her hand up to the back of her head, and winced upon touching the open wound her husband had inflicted. Suddenly grateful for all the gentleman had done for her, she lowered her eyes respectfully. "Thank you, good sir. Please forgive me."

The rescuer smiled and genuinely returned, "Not at all. You are most welcome... And now that I see you are well enough, I will take leave of your chamber for the night."

As he stood up, Samantha blurted, "But I cannot stay here! I must go home! I must go home at once!"

She jumped out of the soft bed, ran out the bedchamber door, down a flight of stairs, and out of a doorway...into the cold darkness.

Chapter 2

When Samantha returned to her little cottage, she found her children—sixteen year old Ethan, and eleven year old Tessa— unharmed.

Tessa asked, "Where have you been, Mumma?"

"Where is your father?" Samantha interjected.

Ethan replied, "He has been away since we woke up. We awoke to his cursing, we heard a door slam, and he was gone... What happened? Where have you been?"

"I prefer not to speak of that. I must instead think...and plan..."

The children respected their mother's wishes. They sat quietly at the kitchen table while Samantha prepared them a late night meal of vegetables and broth.

After they ate, Samantha helped them spread out their bedding by the fireplace. "Please lay down directly, my dear children. Rest your sleepy heads whilst I think."

Several days passed with no sight of Harold. Accustomed to his long absences, the children

9

settled into their normal routine.   Samantha, however, continued to plan a way for the three of them to escape Harold forever.

Unfortunately, all plans held potential for major failure. *If I flee to the home of a relative, Harold might find me and kill me...   He has threatened to kill me many times before, and I have no doubt he would follow through. I cannot bear the thought of my children witnessing their own mother murdered by their father...*

Maybe I could take the children, and escape to some unknown town far away...

No. Her shoulders shrunk. *I have heard of women attempting that before—all outcomes disastrous.   Circumstances usually force the mother to release her children to some ill-reputed orphanage or workhouse. I will take any kind of abuse from Harold before I will allow that to happen!*

No, there seems no alternative but to stay with Harold...and pray. Pray that he might possibly reform, or at the very least, stay away for longer periods of time than he already does.

Chapter 3

One month later, Samantha stepped onto the hilly trail behind her cottage leading to the Painswick town market. She heard the approaching gallop of a horse. A messenger soon appeared. He delivered a letter penned by one Baron John Campbell. It read:

Baron John Campbell, February 16, 1768

My Dearest Lady,

I wonder if you wish to have your night gown returned to you? I will send a messenger on the morrow at the same hour for your response. I have heard word that you are well. I trust that it is so.

Most Sincerely,
John

"Thank you," Samantha said to the messenger.

The messenger tipped his hat, turned his horse, and headed on his backtrack.

Samantha reread the letter more carefully. She nearly dropped the basket which hung over her arm. *Is the messenger still near enough for me to respond now?*

She ran up the hill behind her cottage to see if she could still see him. He had completely disappeared, but the letter remained in her hands. She stared at it in disbelief. *Can this be real—a letter from that fine gentleman who calls me lady?*

She returned to her cottage to hide it.

When the messenger appeared the following day, Samantha gave him a package and a letter of her own. The package contained one clean, neatly-folded nightgown of fine material, assorted homemade rolls, and a small truckle of cheese. Her letter stated:

Honorable Baron Campbell,

Please accept my sincerest gratitude for the care you and your maidservants recently provided me. Please, also,

14

discard the aforementioned article of clothing.

Eternally gratefully yours,

Samantha Talbot

Thank you, dear Lord, Samantha prayed, *for having provided me the ability to read, write, and speak at a level far above most of my peers.*

Before her elderly parents raised her, they had served as house servants to an unusually benevolent duke and duchess. The benevolent duo had allowed—and even encouraged—their servants to be educated in the skills of reading, writing, speaking, and etiquette alongside their own children. Samantha's parents were thus able to educate her before they passed away.

Several days later, Baron Campbell's messenger knocked at the front door of Samantha's cottage. Samantha opened the door, and he handed her a package which she unwrapped immediately. *The same beautiful nightgown I returned to him. I wonder why?*

"A letter accompanies the package, madam," informed the messenger.

She read it.

Baron John Campbell, March 8, 1768

My Dearest Lady,

Please accept this night gown to keep as your own, as no fine lady will look as beautiful in it as you.

Truthfully yours,
John

After the messenger left, Samantha took the package to her bedchamber and closed the door. She put on the nightgown, and happily twirled around. Finally, she sat on the edge of her bed, and fell back on it. *Baron Campbell, you enchant me!*

Suddenly, she heard the backdoor slam. *Harold must have returned!*

As fast as she could, Samantha removed the beautiful nightgown, hid it, and put on her old rags. She entered the kitchen where Harold sat at the table. The chicken broth she had provided the children earlier still steamed, so she served it to him with cheese and a loaf of bread.

After devouring his meal, Harold emptied his tankard of home-brewed ale, belched, and eyed Samantha lasciviously.

"No!" exclaimed Samantha.

Harold stood up, haphazardly knocking his chair to the floor. "Don't you tell me 'No'!" he bellowed.

Before Samantha could flee, Harold stepped forward and grabbed hold of her hair close to her scalp. He dragged her to their bedchamber, and threw her down on the bed.

"No!" Samantha screamed and writhed as Harold pinned her down.

Pulling out the dagger from its sheath on his belt, Harold grabbed hold of her clothing and tore into it.

Fear of being sliced by the formidable object kept Samantha's movements in check. She waited until he finished cutting the clothes from her body, and hurled the dagger to the opposite end of the chamber.

"No, Harold! Please!" she pleaded again.

Harold stood before her, untied the rope holding up his trousers, and allowed them to drop to the floor.

Samantha's eyes bulged in dread when she saw the taut and calloused appendage she knew would soon thrust unmercifully inside her.

Harold grabbed hold of her hair again. This time, he pulled her up and forced her onto the bed face downward, buttocks up.

There is no use. He will have his way with me, regardless... Let him finish and be gone. Samantha held still to wait it out.

Harold thrust his beastly organ deep inside of her again and again until she bled. The sight of Samantha's blood brought forth a demented grunt of contentment from the grimy ogre. He gave one last hard thrust, and grunted lustily while spending himself all over her backside.

Finally, Harold tied up his trousers, staggered out of the bedchamber, and out of the little cottage.

Samantha lay still until she heard the outside door slam behind Harold. *He is on his way. He will not return for a long while.* She exhaled in relief.

Thank you, God, that my children did not hear this. Thank you, for sparing them.

Safely away at their aunt and uncle's home, Ethan and Tessa visited with their cousins.

Chapter 4

Twelve days later, while Samantha gathered wood outside of her cottage, Baron Campbell's messenger delivered the following:

Baron John Campbell, March 20, 1768

My Dearest Lady,

I am told you spend your days with no gentleman present to assist you in your daily endeavors. I wish to humbly offer any service you desire.

Your Obedient Servant,
John

Any service I desire? Is this a trick? Why would anyone of the aristocracy offer such a thing to a common labouring-class woman as myself? Does he think me a whore? I shall not respond to this!

Noting Samantha's glowering countenance, the messenger nervously blurted, "I am ordered to await your response."

Through gritted teeth, Samantha exclaimed, "There will be no response!"

She reentered her cottage, stormed over to her bed, and flopped down upon it in tears completely disheartened. *I had deemed the baron a decent gentleman...only to learn he is most probably scum of the earth!*

She sobbed a long while.

Chapter 5

The following day, after providing her children with their morning lessons and sending them on their way, Samantha heard bells and horses approach from a distance. *Who could that be?*

Waiting curiously at her front door, she dared only to peek out of a small opening. *An elegant coach-and-six!*

The coach with six horses bedazzling in finery stopped nearby, and Baron John Campbell stepped out of it.

No! Samantha quickly shut and locked the door.

The baron knocked.

She refused to answer.

The baron knocked a few more times, and Samantha yelled, "Take leave!"

The baron called through the closed door, "I wish you no harm, my lady! It is only I, John Campbell!"

"I am no common street whore! Take leave, and find one elsewhere!"

The baron froze for a moment, turned on his heels, and returned glumly to his coach.

"Homeward!" he ordered his driver, and the coach-and-six headed back to his estate.

Chapter 6

Baron Campbell sulked for a couple of weeks, but then devised another plan. He chose to arrive more humbly this time—on horseback with only his head house servant, Ichabod.

He and Ichabod soon headed for Samantha's cottage. As they neared the humble abode, the baron heard the loud screams of a female. To his astonishment, he saw a brute of a man swinging a wooden post in the direction of the screaming female.

"No, Harold, please! No!!!" Samantha pleaded as she dodged the swinging post time and time again.

The baron jumped off his horse, ran toward the brute, and drew his sword. Before Harold could swing the wooden post again, Baron Campbell plunged his sword deeply into the offender's fat belly and pulled it back out.

Harold's blood spewed forth, spraying the ground crimson. With a stunned expression, he stumbled forward and fell before Samantha in a heap of jostling flesh.

Dazed, Samantha stared at Harold. She slowly voiced to Baron Campbell, "You've killed him."

"Did you know him?"

Shaking, she stuttered, "He...He... was my husband."

Baron Campbell protested, "But my informants assured me that you... You live alone... You wear no ring... I would not have..."

He stood silently. Then, drawing from his interminable training in the rules of etiquette, he bowed courteously. "My sincerest apologies, madam. I had only seen fit to protect you from whom I had deemed a savage intruder..."

Dumbfounded, Samantha turned away, stepped inside her cottage, and closed the door. Peering through a crack, she watched as Baron Campbell stood staring at the exterminated beast.

Tall and slender Ichabod appeared at his side. "Sir...where might we dispose of the corpse?"

The baron did not respond.

"Shall I find a cart, sir?"

The baron contemplated a moment longer, and affirmed with a nod.

Ichabod secured a cart, and they loaded up Harold's cumbersome remains.

Samantha watched the baron and his servant cart her dead husband away. *Dear Lord, what do I do now?*

An hour later, Samantha heard a knock. From inside her closed front door she asked, "Who is it?"

"It is I, Ichabod—Baron Campbell's premier house servant!"

What could he possibly want of me? Samantha peered out the narrow crack in her door. The servant held a letter in his hands.

She intoned, "Set the letter by the door, and leave!"

Ichabod followed her instructions.

With Ichabod a safe distance away, she opened the door, picked up the letter, and read it.

Baron John Campbell, April 4, 1768

My Dearest Fair Lady,

There are no words sufficient to express the regret I feel. Had I known he was your husband, I assure you I would have addressed the situation in a different manner entirely. I can only express my deepest wish to do my best to assist you in any way possible. I will take care of all funeral arrangements in any way you desire. Please forgive me.

Most sorrowfully,
John

"Wait! Please wait!" Samantha yelled.

Ichabod returned to her, and she said, "Please tell Baron Campbell that I do indeed desire his assistance here presently."

Once informed, Baron Campbell set out for Samantha's cottage with Ichabod. Upon their arrival, they knocked at her door.

That must be the baron! Samantha rushed over to invite them inside. "Please make yourselves comfortable at the kitchen table."

Baron Campbell nodded gratefully, walked across the small cottage to the table, and sat down.

Ichabod followed, and stood nearby.

Samantha served them hot cider, explaining, "If we would hold a funeral for my husband...Harold, I fear word would reach his brother, Ivan. Harold was evil, but Ivan is far more fearsome, cruel, and—worst of all—vengeful. Therefore, I plead with you, for the sake of my family, to keep Harold's death in confidence at all cost."

Baron Campbell earnestly spoke, "You have my word of honor and solemn oath."

"Furthermore," Samantha added, "I plan to keep the truth of what transpired here even from my own children. I shall explain to them that their father died of a hunting accident, and was buried far away."

"It shall be so," the baron responded.

Samantha bowed her head. She rose from her chair, and led the two men out the front door.

Chapter 7

A week later, Samantha received a letter from the baron explaining that he patiently awaited any request she might have for which to make her life more comfortable.

Make my life more comfortable? I have lost my husband! I have no means to support myself and the children!

Samantha did not respond.

Several weeks passed, and the baron sent a reminder letter.

Samantha remained silent.

A few days thereafter, during the late afternoon while her children visited their cousins, Ivan burst into Samantha's cottage fuming, "Where is Harold?"

Samantha's legs nearly gave way beneath her. "He... He's passed away!"

"Where is he?" Ivan's voice boomed.

"He... He's dead!" Samantha's voice shook.

"Who killed him?"

"It... It was an accident—a hunting accident!"

"No! You had him murdered! You had him murdered by your lover, and ye'll pay for this! I'll shred his body, and feed him to the dogs!"

Ivan grabbed and twisted Samantha's arm so brusquely he pulled it from its socket.

Samantha cried out from the torturous pain, and all went black for her.

Ivan left Samantha's unconscious body in a heap, and thundered out of the tiny cottage.

Hours later, when Samantha awoke, she moaned and rolled back and forth on the floor. *My worst fears are being realized!*

She worked her way up a kitchen table leg with her one undamaged arm, and looked around for Ivan. *He must be gone.*

Listening until she felt certain Ivan no longer remained on the premises, she finally cried, "Thank you, God, that I am still alive!"

Holding her injured arm tightly to her body, she headed for her bedchamber. *I must lie down a short while before warning my family. I simply cannot make it right now.*

Shortly after lying down on her bed, the front door burst open. Her Aunt Elizabeth erratically exclaimed, "Samantha! Where are you?"

"In here," Samantha responded weakly.

Aunt Elizabeth yelled to her husband, "She's in her chamber, Charles. Come quick!"

Sitting down next to Samantha, Aunt Elizabeth rattled in a panic, "Darling! Harvey Jenkins brought ill tidings from Painswick Tavern! Harold's brother Ivan is there! Ivan threatens to slay Harold's killer. He swears Painswick will soon be missing one of its most prominent townspeople! What do you know of this?"

Samantha responded lethargically, "I can explain..."

Alarmed anew by Samantha's condition, Aunt Elizabeth frantically inquired, "What has happened here? What has happened to you? Why haven't you told us the truth of Harold's passing?"

Samantha moaned, "Oh dear God! It is worse than a nightmare!"

She sobbed, and then told the full story.

Uncle Charles asserted, "Let us take you away from here and find help! I will go to Baron Campbell, myself. He must know his life is in danger!"

Outside the gate of his estate, Baron Campbell met with Uncle Charles and spoke pensively. "Eternally grateful, my dear man." He reached out his arm, and gripped the shoulder of the kindly, old gentleman.

Uncle Charles offered, "We welcome you to stay at the home of a trusted friend of ours..."

Baron Campbell assured, "That will not be necessary. I have never shrunk from anything before me. I refuse to shrink now. I am prepared to meet this foe face to face."

Uncle Charles said, "Should you have need of assistance, I have friends in the military, who will..."

"I will be fine," the baron interjected. "Please go to your niece and family now. I would have more peace of mind if you remained with them, and saw to their safety."

Uncle Charles bowed his head, and turned to walk away.

Baron Campbell reached his hand out to stop him. "Wait, good sir!"

Uncle Charles turned back towards the baron.

The baron looked him gravely in the eyes. "My sincerest gratitude."

Uncle Charles closed his eyes, nodded, and departed for his home.

Chapter 8

As anticipated, Ivan later appeared at the gate of Baron Campbell's estate.

Upon his guards' notification, the baron left the shelter of his mansion to confront the purported menace.

The guards opened the gate, revealing Ivan's ferocious visage; and the two opponents faced each other.

Ivan snarled, "You *murdered* my brother!"

Stoically, Baron Campbell remained silent. He simply stared at Ivan in the dim light of dusk.

Towering like Goliath over David, Ivan repeated his exclamation more emphatically.

Baron Campbell stared undaunted.

Ivan shook his head, and gutturally warned, "I should kill you right here and now! But, no. I'll take more satisfaction in tearing apart your lover..." He turned and thundered off in the direction of Painswick.

Baron Campbell secured two of his guards to accompany him to the home of Samantha's uncle.

Standing before Charles, the baron described the situation with Ivan. He added, "I respectfully request, sir, that you avail yourself and family to the armament and security of my estate...at least until word arrives that Mistress Talbot's brother-in-law has left the vicinity."

Uncle Charles nodded his assent.

"I shall expect you this evening?" the baron asked hopefully.

"Yes, and gratefully so," affirmed Uncle Charles.

Chapter 9

Maidservants scrambled at Baron Campbell's estate to ready beds for Uncle Charles, Aunt Elizabeth, Samantha, and their combined seven children.

"All prepared, sir," informed Ichabod.

"Wonderful!" acknowledged Baron Campbell, peering out a front window.

Samantha's family made their way down a long private drive, ending with the baron's stonewall. They waited until two guards opened the front gate, and allowed entry.

Once inside, the family stood gawking at the grandeur of the baron's palatial mansion.

My Lord, how regal! Although Samantha had slept under its roof the night the baron rescued her, she had never actually seen the full edifice from the outside.

Built in the extravagant style of French Renaissance architecture, it included one large central gable, two surrounding smaller gables, and two large turrets forming bookends.

"Absolutely breathtaking," whispered Aunt Elizabeth, entranced.

Set against a backdrop of rolling tree-covered hills, the grandiose structure sat above a formal garden featuring Italian white marble statuary and a large pond teeming with swans.

"Look at the ducks!" exclaimed Tessa.

"Those are not ducks. They are swans!" corrected Ethan. "A swan is a status symbol for the wealthy!"

"A status what?" questioned Tessa.

Aunt Elizabeth clarified, "It means Baron Campbell is rich!"

"Come," coaxed Uncle Charles grasping Aunt Elizabeth's arm. "We must see everyone safely inside."

They walked across the grounds.

Baron Campbell greeted them at his front door, and showed them in.

So much more handsome than I recall! For a moment, the immense pain in Samantha's shoulder escaped her mind.

Once inside the mansion, Samantha's family stood with renewed awe. In soft tones, they marveled at the height of the ceiling; the enormity and quantity of rooms; the regality of the Rococo furnishings.

I never noticed any of this whilst I was here before...

"They're here!" announced a child, interrupting Samantha's thought; and several children clomped down a spiral staircase.

He is married?

Aunt Elizabeth inquired, "Are they yours?"

"Yes, madam," the baron replied.

That answers that. Samantha felt disappointed.

"For some reason, I had assumed you had no wife, Baron Campbell," commented Aunt Elizabeth.

"Unfortunately, you assumed correctly," responded the baron.

Aunt Elizabeth appeared perplexed, and Baron Campbell clarified, "My wife passed away one year ago whilst giving birth to our eighth."

Eight children! Samantha swallowed hard while attempting to comprehend the baron's full circumstances.

"I am sorry," Uncle Charles spoke. He bowed his head.

"Thank you, sir," Baron Campbell acknowledged.

"Father!" interrupted one of the baron's older girls. "May we take them upstairs to our bedchambers?"

"Magnificent idea!" Baron Campbell replied, smiling at his children.

The baron's children led the labouring-class children up the spiral staircase. While the boys showed off their wooden toy rifles, ninepins, and dice; the girls displayed their porcelain dolls, stick ponies, and miniature tea sets. The intermingling of all fifteen children created a holiday party atmosphere.

While the children socialized upstairs, Baron Campbell invited the adults to seat themselves in his formal parlor.

Samantha hesitated in the entrance hall just long enough to deliver a short prayer. *Thank You, dear God, for the wonderful sanctuary You have provided for me and my family.*

She entered the parlor and attempted to smile, but her shoulder ached tremendously.

"Mister Daniel Peabody will be here shortly to assist you," the baron explained to her. "Drink some of this. It will help you until he arrives." He handed Samantha a small tankard filled with rum.

Aunt Elizabeth blurted, "But Mister Peabody is the town butcher! How can *he* properly tend to my niece?"

"Do not trouble yourself, good madam," said Baron Campbell. "Mister Peabody is Painswick's only known bonesetter. Doctor Thompson recommended him to me after my second eldest child broke his arm years ago. I attest he did splendid work."

Mister Peabody arrived, and Baron Campbell introduced him.

Only nodding briefly to acknowledge his introduction, Mister Peabody retreated to the entrance hall to speak privately with Baron Campbell. "Best we keep the children well away whilst I work on the lady...so as not to alarm them whilst she screams out in pain." He gave a wink and added, "Ye understand?"

Several feet away, Aunt Elizabeth gaped incredulously at Mister Peabody's toothless smile.

Baron Campbell called the attention of two maidservants. "Make use of the noisemakers I purchased at the fair. Play a game of Blind Man's Bluff or such. Be sure to keep the children well occupied."

The maidservants obediently shuffled off to find the noisemakers.

He returned to the bonesetter, who asked, "Is there a bed, where we might lay the lady down?"

The baron directed him to his own bedchamber on the bottom floor.

With Samantha situated on the baron's bed, Mister Peabody authoritatively stated, "I shall require some assistance..." Pointing to Aunt Elizabeth, he ordered, "You! Hold one of her hands, whilst you," pointing to Uncle Charles, "hold the other!"

As they obeyed, Mister Peabody pulled a bottle and small chalice out of a tired-looking, black leather bag. He poured a brownish liquid into the chalice. "Drink down all these spirits, my good lady," he told Samantha. "You will have need of them."

Samantha willingly drank.

Mister Peabody followed, "I will need you, Baron, to stand behind her and push hard on her shoulder whenst I gives the word."

The baron did as instructed, while the bonesetter positioned himself along Samantha's injured side and grabbed her limp arm.

"Owwwww!" cried Samantha.

"Now, Baron!" bellowed Mister Peabody.

Baron Campbell pushed on Samantha's shoulder while Mister Peabody twisted and pushed Samantha's arm until they heard, "Pop!" The bone had found its way back into its socket before Samantha could cry out again.

As she began to sob softly afterwards, Mister Peabody asked, "How is that?"

Unable to speak, Samantha nodded.

Baron Campbell inquired, "How do you fare?"

Samantha nodded again, and closed her eyes.

Mister Peabody proudly displayed his toothless smile, patted his big belly and said, "She'll be fine. Ye'll all see!"

Fine? I guess it does feel a bit better.
Samantha drifted off to sleep.

The others gathered round the bonesetter to shake his hand and thank him. Baron Campbell gave him a purse of money and extolled, "Fine work, Mister Peabody. Fine work!"

Shaking the money purse lightly to estimate its value; Mister Peabody evinced contentment, nodded farewell, and made way for his exit.

Chapter 10

Three weeks passed with no sight or sound of Ivan. Uncle Charles politely spoke, "Baron Campbell, I feel it is time I take my wife and children home."

"Please feel free to stay as long as you wish," the baron responded.

"I am beyond grateful, Baron. Thank you, but I have obligations to tend to at home."

"Understood." Baron Campbell bowed his head.

Later that day, Uncle Charles, Aunt Elizabeth, and their five children departed from the French Renaissance mansion; while Samantha, Ethan, and Tessa remained.

On a July afternoon a few weeks later, while King George III marked the beaks of his swans for Swan Upping at Windsor Castle, Samantha gazed at the baron's swans from his front terrace. *So majestic and graceful!*

Tessa excitedly ran out onto the terrace, "Mumma, look at me! Bertie made me another new dress!" She twirled around, held out her arms, and hugged Samantha happily. "She is sewing up more clothes for Ethan, too!"

Samantha's daughter ran back into the mansion, passing Baron Campbell as he stepped outside.

When Samantha spotted him, she sincerely spoke, "Thank you, Baron Campbell. Thank you ever so kindly for all you have done for me and the children."

The baron smiled, and his eyes gleamed.

The way he looks at me makes my heart beat wildly! Is it possible I detect love in his eyes? She turned from the baron to shield her face. *What expression must he detect from me? Are my feelings all too apparent?*

Baron Campbell gently spoke, "I am leaving to hunt for a few days. I will take a messenger with me, so as to alert the guards should I see any sign of Ivan whilst I am about."

Samantha mustered her courage, and turned towards him. "Bon chance... Good luck!"

Baron Campbell smiled and approached her. "So you speak French, do you?"

"Un peu... Only a little, Baron Campbell."

"Je m'appelle John," Baron Campbell said.

"Your name is John," Samantha translated proudly.

Baron Campbell looked into her eyes, and spoke seriously. "Yes, and it is about time you started calling me by that name."

Samantha looked down shyly. "Yes sir, Baron Ca—" Looking up she finished, "I mean, yes sir, John."

The baron moved to within inches of Samantha's face. He closed his eyes and inhaled. When he opened them, Samantha stared at him adoringly.

If only he would take me into his arms, and kiss me passionately.

Instead, he kissed her on the cheek. "Au revoir, Belle... Until later, Beautiful."

"Until later...John," Samantha responded.

They stared at each other lovingly, and John finally turned from her and left.

While John hunted, Samantha wondered, *Could he really take interest in a common, labouring-class woman such as myself? I have never heard of such a thing! Maybe he only wishes a permanent caretaker for his children...*

No, he has maidservants who do fine work in that regard.

What if he is hiding something from me? No! I must trust him!

There is something almost magical about him—enchanting!

Chapter 11

After a week, John returned home with a kill to make any hunter proud.

Short and pudgy Isaac, the servant in charge of the kitchen, greeted him outside the mansion and jovially exclaimed, "We'll soon have plenty of delectable venison!" He and another house servant immediately set to work at skinning, quartering, and curing the fresh meat.

John entered his mansion, and asked Ichabod, "Where might I find Mistress Talbot?"

"In the library with the children, sir." He helped John remove his cloak.

Upon finding Samantha, John spied a moment as she told a fable to the children seated around her. He stood still while she finished providing the moral lesson, and then applauded loudly.

All looked over at him, and the children ran to hug him.

Samantha stood up, and smoothed her hair. She pinched her cheeks, and bit her lips to add color. *I must look a mess!*

As the children cleared out, John asked, "How fares my beautiful lady on this magnificent day?"

"Quite content, I am sure!" Samantha responded shyly.

He kissed her cheek and extolled, "You had the children *captivated* whilst you read to them... Just as *I* am captivated by your beauty!"

Samantha excused herself, and scurried upstairs toward her bedchamber. Before entering, she peered over the banister, and noticed John's confused expression as he walked to his own bedchamber.

An hour later, Samantha enjoyed fresh air out on the front terrace. She watched a swan couple coquettishly frolic.

John approached from directly behind her, and softly said, "I apologize if I did something to upset you earlier..."

Samantha turned to look at him.

John continued, "When I told you I was captivated by your beauty; I meant I am not only captivated by your beauty on the *outside*, but more importantly your beauty on the *inside*."

"Thank you, John. But I am the one who needs to apologize to you. You did nothing to offend me. It is only that..." She averted her eyes. "I feel undeserving of your attentions."

Looking into his eyes again, she fervently continued. "You deserve a *real* lady of your *own* class...not a common, labouring-class woman such as myself!"

John grabbed both of her hands, and pulled her close. "No, Samantha. You are neither common nor of a lower class in my eyes. I will not let the townspeople, nor anyone else, dictate my choice... I only want you."

"But," Samantha interjected.

Before she could speak further, John reiterated, "I only want you."

They stood facing each other on the terrace, hands holding hands, eyes staring ardently into eyes.

Samantha finally spoke. "I love you."

John smiled, and embraced her warmly. He grabbed her face, opened his mouth, and kissed her passionately, lovingly.

Interrupting the magical moment, a male voice erratically cried, "Baron Campbell! Baron Campbell!"

John reluctantly pulled away from Samantha. "On the front terrace!"

Isaac found him, and excitedly rattled, "Ivan is on his way here! A small army of Hun-like brutes accompanies him! He promises a week of harlots for your 'capture, humiliation, and destruction'! You must leave at once!"

John grabbed hold of Isaac's arms in an attempt to settle him down. "How do you know this? Who informed you?"

"Ichabod!" Isaac responded, still wildly erratic. "Ichabod confessed it was he who told Ivan you killed Samantha's husband! He said Ivan promised a purse of gold! But Ivan refused to pay...."

John brusquely spoke, "Where is Ichabod now?"

"He ran out the kitchen door towards the back gate of the estate! Shall I go after him for you?"

"No!" John paused. He firmly added, "God will judge him, and serve him his just rewards. We must take care of ourselves now... Does Ivan resolve to hurt Mistress Talbot or her children?"

"I do not know!" blubbered the house servant, sinking down regretfully.

John lifted Isaac to straighten him. "Regardless, we need to move everyone to safety. We must leave before nightfall. Round up the servants for their immediate assistance."

"Yes, sir!" said Isaac, composing himself rapidly and rushing off to follow instructions.

Chapter 12

Preparations complete, John's horse-drawn carriages headed to his older half-brother's estate at Stow-on-the-Wold, the highest town of the Cotswolds. After a full night and half-day of travel, John pointed up a steep hill. "There it is!"

Through a clearing in the trees, they saw the enormous Gothic-Revival styled mansion with its intricately-detailed, castellated parapet roof.

"How elegant!" exclaimed Samantha.

Sir Peter and his wife Lady Cornwall soon greeted them at the door. Customarily much more formal than his younger half-brother, Sir Peter wore a blue velvet suit (coat, waistcoat, and breeches) decorated with gold braid and buttons. His waistcoat revealed a white shirt with ruffled cravat to match his white wig and stockings. Black shoes exhibited two-inch heels.

Lady Cornwall wore a courtly, pale blue, full-length gown. Her sleeves and underskirt exhibited several layers of flounces trimmed with white lace. Like Sir Peter, she also wore a white wig, but hers stood much taller and displayed strings of pearls and a large plume.

Samantha's eyes gaped. *Truly amazing!*

"Welcome! Welcome, everyone!" exclaimed Sir Peter with open arms.

Lady Cornwall stood silently nearby with an unaffected countenance.

"I see my messenger informed you of our situation," John said. "I hope you can forgive our intrusion!"

"Not at all, my good brother! Susan and I have been *lonesome* since our own children removed themselves from here. We are more than pleased to have your company!"

Samantha suddenly sensed a feeling of foreboding. *Something evil resides here.*

She shook it off as John introduced her and her two children.

Lady Cornwall said to Samantha, "Come. Let us make ourselves comfortable."

Samantha followed along to a formal parlor, where Lady Cornwall gestured for her to sit down. Mesmerized by the red velvet curtains, chairs, and table cloth; Samantha missed her cue.

"Sit down," Lady Cornwall instructed verbally this time.

Samantha obeyed.

Thanks be to God I wear the dress John provided me! She wore one of his late wife's formal gowns. *Lady Cornwall's apparel is utterly stunning!*

A kitchen servant entered to serve tea and crumb cake using dainty white porcelain tea cups, saucers, and cake plates.

Samantha remarked, "I am absolutely enamored of your gown, Lady Cornwall! Please tell me about it."

With an imperious tone of voice—strongly emphasizing a rolling r, Lady Cornwall explained, "This gown originates from *Austria*—although I recently purchased several similar gowns in *France*. The particular beauty I wear today is made of *genuine silk*. There is nothing on earth so soft to the touch..." She proudly ran her hand along the material to display it.

Samantha listened respectfully while Lady Cornwall continued. "In keeping with *this* season's fashion, you may clearly see that my underskirt is of the identical *exquisite* material."

Lady Cornwall eyed Samantha's gown up and down critically.

Samantha looked down at the gown she wore. *Oh my! This gown is more beautiful than any I have ever worn before, but it is not of today's fashion!* Her underskirt completely contrasted in color and texture with the overgown. *How embarrassing!*

Lady Cornwall ran her hand up the side of her tall wig, and stroked her plume adornment as if begging for a compliment.

Shaking off her embarrassment, Samantha commented sweetly, "Your feather is admirable. From what type of bird is it?"

Presenting an incredulous visage, Lady Cornwall spoke condescendingly. "My what??? Oh, you must mean my *plume*. This *plume* is a genuine ostrich *plume*. I purchased it the last time Sir Peter and I visited friends of ours in *Paris*."

With a sudden shift in attitude, Lady Cornwall surveyed the parlor from left to right. She raised up her dress to the level slightly above her ankles. Under her many layers of petticoats, Samantha saw elegant silk stockings and a unique pair of high-heeled shoes completely covered with colorfully embroidered taffeta. "Feast your eyes on my pompadour heels before the gentlemen

72

enter! Sir Peter is unaware of this purchase, as it is one of the many items I acquired after his request I stop my spending. These shoes are the *envy* of *all my lady friends."*

Suddenly ringing a bell, Lady Cornwall rasped, "More tea! *More tea!"*

A servant quickly entered the parlor, and poured more tea into their cups.

Samantha sipped her tea. *There it is again— that feeling of foreboding.* She noticed hair standing up on her arms. *I must not let her know I am troubled!* She quickly changed her expression from worried to interested, but noticed that the self-obsessed Lady Cornwall babbled on completely unaware.

While Lady Cornwall incessantly boasted, the children, using their best manners, stood quietly inside the entrance hall where medieval suits of armor and coats of arms held their attention.

Finally, Sir Peter announced, "Well, children, let us go out to the barn to see what we might find there!"

"Hurray!" the children cheered while running outside.

Sir Peter lit his pipe before following the children with John. Stopping halfway between the house and barn, he commented matter-of-factly, "Samantha's a beauty." He puffed once on his pipe, and turned to meet his brother's eyes.

John smiled. "Yes, and what amazes me is she is even more so on the in...."

"She's of the labouring-class!" Sir Peter interjected sharply.

"I am fully apprised of that," John responded.

Sir Peter's eyes veered away. He puffed his pipe, and continued on to the barn.

While the younger children busied themselves petting the cows, horses, pigs, goats, and sheep; the two eldest children—Samantha's Ethan and John's Adam—organized the construction of a mountain of hay.

Ethan soon announced, "The mountain is ready!"

Samantha's eleven-year-old Tessa ran up the pile of hay laughing happily all the way.

Ten-year-old William yelled at her, "Hey, get off of that mountain! Girls can't play King of the Mountain!"

"Come on up, and try to knock me off of it.... I dare you!" Tessa challenged.

William took the bait, and ran up the pile of hay. Reaching the top, he and Tessa locked arms. Tessa pushed with all her might until William slid down a ways from the top. Finally, with Tessa's unyielding force, William lost his footing completely and fell face-first into the hay.

Quickly returned to the top of the hay, Tessa raised her arms victoriously. "I'm king of the mountain!"

All of the children laughed.

Sir Peter grinned. "It appears William has met more than his match!"

John steadfastly agreed.

A short while later, a kitchen servant summoned everyone for dinner putting an end to all of the fun. Sir Peter escorted the hungry children to the mansion's banquet hall, where servants had set a long, thick, walnut table with fine silver dinnerware and candlesticks.

As the children seated themselves, John caught sight of Samantha, who appeared shy and disconcerted. He approached her, and kissed her cheek.

Samantha blushed and smiled.

Sir Peter noticed the encounter, and spoke hurriedly, "Come! The adults eat in the formal dining room!"

Towards the end of an uncomfortably quiet dinner, Lady Cornwall suddenly announced, "I am utterly *fatigued*. I must retire to my bedchamber at once, or I fear I will be left wanting for beauty sleep..."

John and Samantha glanced at each other, and briefly smiled. Their expressions conveyed, "Well, Lady Cornwall, then you should have been asleep long ago!" Lady Cornwall's lack of *inner* beauty strongly affected their opinion of her outer appearance.

Shortly after Lady Cornwall had withdrawn to her bedchamber—located on the opposite end of the mansion from Sir Peter's—Sir Peter announced, "Come! I will show you and the children to your sleeping accommodations!"

Sleeping accommodations! Samantha looked at John. *Would that my bedchamber were the same as John's!*

Sir Peter ushered everyone upstairs to their bedchambers. Samantha's chamber sat between John's and the children's.

Not surprisingly, we will not be sharing a bed... But at least he sleeps nearby. Samantha stepped inside her chamber, and inspected the beautiful Gothic furnishings.

A few minutes later, Samantha put on her nightgown and brushed her hair. Looking into a mirror, she caught sight of the bed located behind her. *Would that John could join me this night.*

Meanwhile, John left his chamber to tuck the children into their beds. Returning through the upstairs hall, he stepped in front of Samantha's bedchamber as she stepped out; and they collided.

Barely stifling a squeal, Samantha exclaimed, "Oh, please forgive me! I had only wished to tuck the children into bed."

"No need, my dear," John smiled. "I have already done so. They are almost fast asleep as we speak... But how fortunate for me that you stepped out, as I had desired to speak with you privately... You appeared unsettled before dinner.

Did Susan treat you unkindly, or has anything upset you?"

"No," Samantha averted her eyes to conceal the truth. "I must have been a wee bit tired. That is all."

John moved closer to Samantha.

She looked up, and with noses almost touching, they stared deeply into each other's eyes.

Inhaling, Samantha savored his manly scent. The twinge of desire throbbed between her legs. *If only I could embrace you, and never let go! I would take you to my bed and...*

John embraced Samantha tenderly. He opened his mouth to kiss her, but froze when he heard his brother call from downstairs.

"John!" Sir Peter repeated from the bottom of the staircase.

"Damn," said John. He pulled Samantha close, and whispered into her ear, "Good night, Beautiful."

Samantha gasped upon feeling his warm, moist breath. Quickly regaining composure, she whispered, "Good night, Handsome."

John kissed Samantha swiftly on the cheek, and headed down the staircase. "Coming, Peter..."

"Would you care to join me for a brandywine?" Sir Peter asked.

"Please," John affirmed.

Sir Peter poured John a brandy, and they toasted to brotherhood. They chatted awhile, and finally retired to their bedchambers for the night.

Chapter 13

The next day, John awoke early to find his half-brother stoking a fire in the largest fireplace of the mansion, downstairs in the dance hall.

Sir Peter, already having donned his formal attire, turned and saw John approach. Evincing consternation, he admonished, "My dear brother, why on earth do neither you nor any of your party sport a wig? Many in the lower class now sport them. One appears *absolutely naked* without one!"

"Peter, I have *always* been a fish swimming against the current. You must be accustomed to it by now... I am no different than my dear, departed father. You recall his habitual comment..."

Sir Peter nodded dismally, and turned his back towards John.

Imitating his father's voice, John continued. "I am of the opinion that wigs make men look like the rows of pots displayed on the apothecary's shelves. Like those pots, wigs are much ornamented, but *always* stand empty."

Sir Peter continued to stoke the fire. Over his shoulder, he said, "Yes, John. I recall... I respected our dear mother's husband—your father.

But things have progressed since then... Be advised that on the morrow, Sunday, as we attend church, Lady Cornwall and I may have to seat ourselves a fair distance from the likes of you!"

A cheerful female voice broke the tension. "Good morrow, good fellows!"

The brothers turned towards the voice to see Samantha gliding down the central staircase. She wore another of John's late wife's spectacular gowns.

"Samantha, you are absolutely radiant! I take it you slept well?"

"Yes I did. Thank you, John!" she beamed.

Sir Peter grumbled under his breath.

"What's that you say, Peter?" John inquired.

Sir Peter spoke sarcastically. "Nothing, *Baron Campbell!* Nothing at all!" He threw down his fireplace poker, and marched out the front door in a huff.

Samantha's face turned scarlet as she said, "I believe Sir Peter would prefer that I address you more formally. I will do so henceforth!"

"No, Samantha. Peter must accustom himself to it, and he will!"

Samantha spoke gently, "I beg your pardon, John, but I would feel more comfortable addressing you as Baron Campbell in Sir Peter's presence—seeing that he *is* allowing me and my children to impose upon this magnificent residence of his."

Regaining composure, John conceded. "Very well, Beautiful... But only if you promise to call me by my given name in private." He winked at her.

"I promise!" Samantha buoyantly spoke.

John smiled and asked, "Now, may I kiss your irresistible cheek, *Samantha?*"

"Yes, you may...*John.*" Samantha smiled while tilting her cheek towards him.

Unbeknownst to John and Samantha, Lady Cornwall had entered the room and witnessed their interchange. "Peter! Peter, where *are* you?" she hysterically shrieked.

John turned toward Lady Cornwall and facetiously spoke, "Good Lord, Susan! Is a rat chewing on your leg?"

Appearing flabbergasted, Lady Cornwall did not respond.

More serious, John said, "Peter has stepped outside momentarily. Could I be of service?"

"Ohhhh! I need Sir Peter!" Lady Cornwall whined. "Baron Campbell, please go tell him *I need him!*"

John gave Samantha an apologetic look, and she sweetly coaxed, "Go ahead, J- ; I mean, go ahead, *Baron Campbell.*"

After John left the building, Samantha turned toward Lady Cornwall. "Good morrow, Lady Cornwall."

Lady Cornwall indignantly shook her head. Turning to a nearby house servant, she instructed, "Tell Sir Peter he shall find me in the 'drawing room!"

How degrading, thought Samantha. *I shall never fit in with the upper class. Who am I fooling? What is John thinking?*

Chapter 14

The following morning, as John, Samantha, and the children stood in the entrance hall ready for church; Lady Cornwall, in the withdrawing room, screeched from the top of her lungs. "No, Peter! We *cannot* let our neighbors know they are guests of ours! We will be *laughingstocks!* Without wigs, they appear *vile heathens!*"

Dear Lord! Samantha shifted uneasily. Her skin prickled with discomfort. *I have never felt such rejection!*

Shortly after Lady Cornwall's ranting polemic, Sir Peter appeared before the stunned group. He solemnly spoke, "Please proceed to church without us... Lady Cornwall is not feeling well today, and I must stay home to tend to her. Hurry along now so as not to be late."

John stoically nodded to his brother, and opened the door to let everyone out. Once outside, he attempted to cheer everyone up with, "Let us go quickly before Lady Cornwall's *disease* catches one of us!" He held out his hands as though they were the claws of an evil witch.

The children played along, running and screaming "Ahhhhhhhhhhhhh!" while John chased them all the way to the horse-drawn carriages.

Samantha's eyes sparkled as she laughed aloud. Seating herself next to John, she grabbed hold of his arm and exclaimed, "Life with you is jolly good fun!"

John kissed her cheek, smiled, and called to the lead driver, "To St. Edward's Church!"

The carriages arrived at St. Edward's just as the church bells began to sound. "St. Edward's boasts the loudest bells in all of Gloucestershire!" John shouted to Samantha. "This church has been here since the 12th century!"

Samantha smiled while looking up at the bell tower. She nodded her understanding.

As John, Samantha, and the children entered St. Edward's and took their seats in the pews, Samantha noticed increasing stares, nudging, and whispering. *Oh my! We truly are the only ones without wigs!* She reached up and touched her own hair as she looked questioningly at John.

He smiled, winked at her, and whispered, "Do not trouble your pretty head. You and the children are *perfect!*"

Samantha felt better, and turned her attention toward the priest, who welcomed everyone and initiated the Sunday worship service.

After church, they returned to Sir Peter's mansion where the aroma of baked chicken, carrots, and potatoes cheerfully welcomed them inside. Since Sir Peter and the irascible Lady Cornwall kept to themselves, John and Samantha dined with the children in the banquet hall.

"Mumma, why did everyone stare at us and whisper?" Tessa asked aloud.

Samantha deferred to John, who responded, "There are customs some people follow, which I feel make no sense. For example, the custom of sporting a wig... I see no good reason for it. Wigs are hot, they itch, and they make a person grow bald. I have chosen for my family *not* to sport them... I say, 'Dare to be different!' If someone should shun me for my ways, then I need him *not* as a friend!"

Samantha smiled gratefully and added, "Moreover, if one does not attempt to try new things, one's mind might forever remain as stationary as those who lived during the Dark Ages."

John winked at Samantha. "That's my lady!" he exclaimed.

He is pleased! How wonderful that we think alike! Samantha took a bite of her chicken, joining the others in happily consuming the bountiful Sunday dinner.

After dinner, Sir Peter entered the banquet hall and cheerfully announced, "Stow-on-the-Wold, where the wind blows cold! That is what we Stow natives say!"

John commented, "The cold is well and good, but it rains this noon..."

Sir Peter continued, "And that is why I am here to declare, 'Come one, come all to the game hall!' It is time we engage ourselves in some of my favorite pastimes!"

Realizing that rain meant no outside play, the children cheered at the prospect of new indoor activities. They stood up, leaving the dirty dishes to the servants, and followed Sir Peter to the game hall.

A crackling fire roared inside, inviting everyone to enjoy a cozy day of indoor fun.

Sir Peter announced, "The first activity I will demonstrate hides under this coverlet. It is my pride and joy!"

Everyone gathered round, and Sir Peter lifted the coverlet.

John's oldest, Adam, exclaimed, "A new billiard table!"

The children's eyes opened admiringly, and John said, "Quite a handsome one at that! Children, did you know that long, long ago in Old England billiards was played out on the grass? Yes, and when the royalty wished to bring the game indoors, the billiard table with its grass-green cloth was invented!"

Samantha's Ethan asked, "Baron Campbell?"

"Yes, Ethan?"

"Can we play now?"

John laughed. "Okay, no further history lessons today. Please, Peter, demonstrate for us how it is played."

While the children and gentlemen contented themselves with the billiard table, Samantha spied the mansion's library across the way. *Vacant!*

She tiptoed over there.

Inside, a flickering fire beckoned her to relax on a chaise longue near the fireplace to enjoy a leisurely day of reading. *Heavenly!*

She sat down to warm her toes and read.

The sounds of merriment emanating from the game hall embraced her like a comforting blanket. She sighed contentedly. *A nearly perfect day!*

Later that evening, in one of the bedchambers, Samantha finished reading a story to the children. "And that is how Sir Thomas, Lady Amanda's handsome and virile knight-in-shining-armor, saved his beautiful damsel-in-distress!"

Amanda affirmed, "That story pleases me!"

"It does me, too," Samantha agreed with a grin. "Now, off to bed, all of you!"

"Aw! We want to hear another story," whined Tabitha.

"Yes, another story," added Sarah.

Samantha shook her head. "No, it is time I tuck you all into bed. Dreamland awaits!"

The children went to their beds, and awaited Samantha's goodnight kiss.

As she tucked Tessa into bed, Tessa grabbed hold of her arm and whispered, "Mumma, why do you call Uncle Peter, 'Sir Peter' and his wife 'Lady Cornwall'?"

"Because, darling, Uncle Peter is a knight. He has earned that privilege. Sir Peter's wife is called Lady Cornwall because that is how one addresses the wife of a knight. Cornwall is Sir Peter's surname."

Tessa whispered, "How did Uncle Peter become a knight?"

"I have not yet learned the answer to that. We must address that question to Baron Campbell."

Samantha started to exit the room, but Tessa pulled her mother close again. "Mumma, if you marry Baron Campbell, what would we call *you?*"

Samantha laughed softly. "Well, you, of course, may always call me Mumma. But..." She smiled dreamily, face upward a moment. "Others would call me *Baroness.*"

"Oh, how beautiful and *enchanting!*" remarked Tessa.

Samantha looked Tessa directly in the eyes and affirmed, "*Love* is enchanting, my daughter."

Tessa's eyes twinkled.

Suddenly serious, Samantha said, "All right, you. That will be all tonight! Sweet dreams, my sweet girl!"

With that, she kissed Tessa's forehead and exited the room.

Chapter 15

The next morning after breakfast, Lady Cornwall left the mansion to meet with her lady friends; Sir Peter met with his accomptant in the gallery; and Samantha commenced the children's morning recitations in the dance hall.

Four-year-old twins Henry and Rachel stood up and recited, "Four farthings make one penny. Twelve pennies make one shilling."

"Good!" praised Samantha, and the twins sat down proudly.

Six-year-old Tabitha said, "They forgot to tell you that pence means more than one penny! We count one penny, two pence, three pence, four."

"That's right, Tabitha. Excellent! Now, Tabitha, how many shillings make one pound?"

William stood up and blurted out, "Twenty! There are twenty shillings in a pound!"

Samantha teased William, "Is your name Tabitha?"

"No, Mistress Talbot." William's face pinked, and he sat down.

Tabitha grinned.

Before Samantha could quiz Tabitha and the older children, John entered the hall. "How fortunate we are to have such wonderfully behaved, intelligent children!"

The children beamed, and John said, "Samantha, may I have a word with you?"

She nodded her head, and followed him into the entrance hall. Once there, she asked, "Yes?"

John stepped close to her. "I only wish to tell you that you are performing miracles with the children... *Thank you.*" He stared desirously into her eyes.

Samantha stared in return, equally desirous. She licked her lips. *Please kiss me!*

John licked his lips, and moved to kiss Samantha's mouth; but the sound of something crashing and breaking in the dance hall interrupted him.

"Kathryn!" screamed the children. "Kathryn broke Lady Cornwall's vase! Bad, Kathryn!"

By the time John and Samantha returned to the dance hall, one-year-old Kathryn stood crying amongst the porcelain remains of one of Lady Cornwall's prized possessions.

Samantha scooped Kathryn into her arms, and melodiously comforted, "You are all right, my little kitten. It is *all right.*"

Holding on tightly, John's youngest child laid her head on Samantha's shoulder and quieted down.

Meanwhile, John left to find a house servant to clean up the rubble. Upon his return with a servant, he whispered to Samantha, "Carry on, Beautiful," and exited the dance hall.

"What a *lovely* time I had with *my lady friends!*" pierced Lady Cornwall's shrill voice through the sound of whirring wind as she entered the front door.

Oh dear! The old shrew is home!

Samantha took it as a cue to end the morning lessons. "That will be all for today, children. You are free to play outside!"

"Hurray!" they cheered, jumping up and running for the front door like a herd of elephants. On their way, they nearly knocked down Lady Cornwall, who stared at them indignantly.

While the last child shut the outside door, the incensed woman screamed, "Wild animals! Watch your steps!"

Ugh! I should have waited 'til she vacated the entrance hall. Samantha sighed. *I will not make that mistake again...*

Gertrude, Lady Cornwall's favorite servant, assisted with the removal of her cloak as the overwrought woman complained, "Vile *heathens!* That is what *they* are! *Despicable!*"

Samantha stepped into the entrance hall. "Good day, Lady Cornwall."

Lady Cornwall glared icily at Samantha. She pursed her lips and sniveled to Gertrude, "I have a sick headache. I will take my chamomile tea in my bedchamber!"

"Yes'm, m'Lady Sue," purred Gertrude devotedly.

Samantha could only watch with gaping eyes as Lady Cornwall marched across the mansion, and out of sight. Looking down at her arms, she realized, *There go the goosebumps again.*

John appeared. "I guess *now* is not the appropriate time to tell Susan about her precious vase?"

Caught by surprise, Samantha laughed and agreed, "No, now is not the time!"

Chapter 16

At midday a few weeks later, Lady Cornwall returned to the mansion refreshed from another lady friends visit. After she passed the gallery, John commented, "Susan seems to really enjoy her time away."

Sir Peter nodded.

John continued, "I wonder if she might allow Samantha to accompany her...on the morrow?"

Sir Peter stared sardonically at John. "Are you cognizant of what you propose?"

John adamantly replied, "I am *fully* aware, or I would not ask it. It would do Samantha good to socialize with those of the female persuasion. She is long overdue for a respite from the children."

"Very well," Sir Peter relented. "But I cannot promise the results to be positive...and that is *even if* Lady Cornwall assents to Samantha accompanying her."

"Cursed wench!" fumed Lady Cornwall to Sir Peter as Gertrude massaged her neck. "The ladies would *excommunicate* me! Invite someone of the labouring-class? A commoner? *Deplorable!"*

After Lady Cornwall finished her scornful tirade, Sir Peter said, "I only ask you to think on it, my dear." He closed the door to the withdrawing room.

Upon his return to the gallery, John asked, "So?"

Sir Peter replied, "There is a fair chance."

Meanwhile, back at the withdrawing room, Gertrude continued massaging Lady Cornwall's neck while whispering into her ear.

After listening intently, Lady Cornwall displayed a mischievous visage. One eyebrow rose high, and her eyes gleamed demonically. When she spoke, her words methodically spilled forth. "Yes... yes, Gertrude, my love. Magnificent idea."

She turned towards Gertrude, pulled her close, and kissed her fully on the mouth...and she did not cease for quite a while.

Chapter 17

Sir Peter informed John the following morning that Lady Cornwall awaited Samantha to accompany her on her lady friends visit.

Samantha, already at work, thanked John for his thoughtfulness. She dismissed the children, and hurried to her bedchamber to ready herself.

Dear Lord, how ever shall I dress? All upper class ladies? Dear me! I am completely benumbed!

No! I cannot let any of them know it—especially not Lady Cornwall!

A few moments later, she walked trepidatiously down the main staircase. She overheard Lady Cornwall rasp, "Tell her I await her in my phaeton!"

John responded, "Very well."

As the front door closed behind Lady Cornwall, John turned and saw Samantha. He gasped; but before he could compliment her, she asked, "What on God's earth is a phaeton?"

John chuckled. "Merely a flowery word for a small carriage." He swiftly kissed her cheek.

A maidservant assisted her with her cloak, and opened the door.

Samantha could now see the elaborately adorned phaeton. "How charming!"

She hurried towards the phaeton; and with the help of the footman, stepped inside and seated herself next to Lady Cornwall.

Without acknowledging Samantha, Lady Cornwall shouted to her driver, "Carry on! We are late!"

Dear me! I can only hope Lady Cornwall's lady friends are nothing like her! Samantha turned her head away from Lady Cornwall to look out the window.

The phaeton took off rapidly for the home of Lady Zelda Cobham, Lady Cornwall's sister. They sped along a winding road past several thatched-roof homes of honey-colored stone. At the top of a hill, they saw the colossal mansion of Palladian architecture—built with the standard front portico supported by four columns.

Lady Zelda Cobham stood under the portico near the entrance doorway with an artificial smile plastered on her face. "Good *morrow*, Mistress Priscilla! Don't you look *scrumptious* today?"

After Mistress Priscilla entered, Lady Cobham rolled her eyes. She composed herself for the next guest, doled out a similar false compliment, and again appeared displeased once the guest vacated the portico for the interior.

Servant girls directed the ladies to beautifully embroidered, taffeta-covered chairs in a formal parlor. They helped them remove their cloaks, gloves, and hats; taking the items away to a cloakroom.

After a servant girl ushered Samantha to her seat and poured her some imported black tea, the catty talk began. Groups of two or three ladies huddled gossiping over painted porcelain plates and teacups, pinkies out.

I feel so isolated! Samantha peered around the room.

Lady Cornwall remained under the portico with her sister, which left Samantha with no one to introduce her.

Staring at the floor, she listened and blushed as she overheard smidgeons of conversation:

"Who is *she*, and where is her *wig?*" Lady Margaret inflected snobbishly.

Mistress Minthrope cackled, "She is Lady Cornwall's company. The *labouring-class* woman!"

"She is very pretty!" enthused Lady Countess Marissa.

"Quite pretty, I am sure!" agreed Lady Countess Josephine.

"Did someone say she is of the *labouring-class?*" gasped Lady Beatrice.

"A commoner?"

"Why is she here?"

"Who invited her?"

"She doesn't belong."

"No, she doesn't belong!"
"*SHE DOESN'T BELONG!*"

At that point, Lady Zelda Cobham entered the room, and ostentatiously orated with the same pretentious, trilled-r accent as her sister's. "Ladies! Ladies! Welcome and good morrow! I am proud to present to you on this fine, fine day the latest addition to my collection of *priceless* paintings. Please! Feast your eyes on this!" With both arms, Lady Cobham gestured towards a life-sized oil painting of herself.

"Is this not the most *magnificent* likeness you have ever feasted on with your very own eyes? Simply *magnificent*, if I dare say so myself!"

What no one truly dared to say was that the painting portrayed Lady Cobham as at least tenfold more beautiful than reality proved.

After an uncomfortable moment of silence, Lady Countess Josephine provided a courtesy lie. "An exact likeness, to be sure, Lady Cobham!"

"Yes...to be sure!" Lady Countess Marissa assisted.

Lady Zelda Cobham smiled pleasurably while extolling, "Thank you my *dear girls!*"

She promenaded proudly to her full length mirror, admired her reflection, and sat down on a chair which resembled a throne.

Raising her head pompously, she continued, "Now, ladies, my lovely daughter Jezebel will demonstrate for you the latest in ballet dance positions! She acquired this knowledge during her most *recent excursion* to *Paris*. Come, Jezebel, my sweet, *beautiful* girl!"

On cue, seventeen-year-old Jezebel entered the parlor and sauntered around the room on tiptoe exhibiting the latest in Parisian ballet costumes. Thin and tall like Lady Zelda Cobham, she raised one sticklike leg out to her side, and then straight up so that her toe pointed flawlessly to the ceiling.

The *ladies* applauded, calling out, "Encore! Encore!"

Energized by their enthusiasm, Jezebel sauntered to a different vantage point in the parlor. She stopped, and posed again. This time, she stood on one leg with one arm extended in front, the other leg and arm extended behind. She proudly proclaimed, "In *Paris*, one calls this the *arabesque!*"

The ladies applauded again.

I am so relieved. Samantha relaxed more comfortably in her chair. *The focus of attention is on her and not me!*

While Jezebel continued to saunter and pose, Mistress Priscilla sipped her tea and whispered to Mistress Minthrope, "Tea is becoming ruinously expensive nowadays!"

Mistress Minthrope's eyes protruded as she grabbed hold of the apron of the next servant girl to walk by.

"Yes'm, may I 'elp ye?" asked the girl.

Mistress Minthrope cackled, "Keep my cup filled with tea, and there'll be a farthing in it for ye."

"Yes'm."

The servant girl went to the kitchen, and facetiously said to a friend, "One old 'ag, she promises me a whole bloomin' farthing for keepin' 'er tea cup filled. What do ye think o' that?"

"Me thinks that ye must *keep* the old 'ag's cup filled. But be sure ye fill it with some o' this 'ere *special* tea!" She winked, and scraped up some mouse droppings from the base of the floor. She tossed them into the teapot, and swirled it around.

The servant girl laughed, and happily returned to Mistress Minthrope with the altered tea.

Jezebel finally finished her performance, and Lady Zelda Cobham called out, "Ladies, tell me what you think of *my scones!* Are they not the most *delectable* and *delicious delights* you have ever *tasted?*"

"Yes, Lady Cobham," agreed Lady Constance. "What did your baker use in them?"

"I *knew* someone would ask this!" Lady Zelda Cobham imperiously responded. "My baker uses currants, lemon curd, and a *spot* of clotted cream. Are they not the most *delectable delights* you have *ever tasted?*"

"Delectable!" agreed Lady Countess Marissa, winking secretively at Lady Countess Josephine, who added, "Delightful!" and smiled back at her friend.

"Why thank you, girls," said Lady Zelda Cobham. She added, "And Lady Marissa, I believe you will be hosting next. Is that right?"

"Yes!" exclaimed Lady Countess Marissa. "You are all invited to my residence, where I will be serving my baker's new miniature teacake recipe. She calls them *hobnobs!*" She smiled proudly.

The ladies responded with gleeful chatter while rising from their chairs and waiting for the servant girls to retrieve their outer apparel.

Upon receiving her items, Samantha slipped out the front door, and hurried over to the phaeton.

Whew! I am glad to have that *behind me!* She closed her eyes in an effort to shut out the pernicious events of the Cobham residence while awaiting Lady Cornwall.

Lady Cornwall arrived several minutes later, and entered the phaeton with the help of her footman. "Hurry home!" she commanded. "I must take my beauty nap at once!"

The driver did as instructed, and they soon returned home without a word spoken.

Chapter 18

The next morning, John informed Samantha that Lady Cornwall again awaited her.

Samantha spoke diplomatically. "I fear the children will fall behind with their lessons. Please explain to Lady Cornwall for me, will you?"

John gazed adoringly into her eyes. "As you wish, my love."

You are wonderful, John! Samantha stared admiringly at him. *Thank you for rescuing me from that crowd of vainglorious fanatics!*

She simply smiled at him, and went back to work.

Later that morning, Lady Cornwall returned from Lady Countess Marissa's, and marched straight into the gallery announcing, "I have *extremely* agreeable news for you, Baron Campbell!"

"Speak!" John responded, evincing interest.

"The daughter of someone *very special* has made it known that she wishes for you to *court her!*"

Sir Peter jovially teased, "Tell us *who*, my dear. You hold us in suspense!"

"With pleasure! The *someone special* is my very own dear sister, Lady Zelda Cobham; and the prospective candidate for Baron Campbell's courtship is of course, her daughter, my niece...*Jezebel!*"

John inwardly shuddered at the sight of Lady Cornwall's smile, which appeared larger than he had ever seen before.

"Oh, I could not be happier!" Lady Cornwall continued. "What a *magnificent* pairing you two will make!"

She proceeded to exit the room, and John's emphatic response halted her mid-exit. "No, Susan. There will be no such pairing. Please make it clear to your sister and niece. Make sure they understand it is impossible."

Lady Cornwall incredulously faced the gentlemen. "Peter, *explain* to him. *See* that he changes his mind." With upturned nose, she turned again and completed her exit.

Sir Peter appeared grave for a moment. "Let us go for a walk, shall we?"

"Let us walk," agreed John, and they headed out of the gallery and out the front door of the Gothic mansion.

Several yards down the long driveway, Sir Peter completed his dissertation. "I only ask you to think on it, my dear brother.   Think on it overnight, and we will discuss it on the morrow,"

"There is nothing on which to think," John responded.   "You must realize and accept that my heart belongs to Samantha…   I wish to have no other."

Sir Peter adamantly repeated, "We will discuss it on the morrow."   He about-faced, and returned to his mansion.

Chapter 19

The brothers awoke earlier than usual the next morning, and met at the main fireplace in the dance hall. Sir Peter spoke first, "Well?"

John feigned a puzzled expression.

Sir Peter continued, "Well, have you thought on it. May I inform Lady Cornwall that you have decided to court Mistress Jezebel?"

"I thought I had made it abundantly clear that I did not require time to think on it," John asserted. "My mind is made up. My heart belongs to Samantha."

Turning to a nearby maidservant, John instructed, "My cloak, if you please."

The servant retrieved John's cloak. He grabbed it, and headed outdoors.

Minutes later, Lady Cornwall visited Sir Peter in his gallery. "So what shall I tell my sister?" she confidently asked. "Shall I set up an evening dinner party for the four of us?"

"Tell her there will be no courting."

Lady Cornwall inhaled vocally until her face turned red. She stomped her foot like a spoiled child and sniveled, "But why not? What reason? Tell me *why!*"

Sir Peter resignedly said, "My brother has informed me that his heart belongs to the labouring-class woman...Samantha. He will court no other."

Lady Cornwall's mouth simply dropped open, and her eyes bulged. Gertrude assisted her with her cloak; and, with a dumbfounded countenance, Lady Cornwall stumbled outdoors to her phaeton.

Shortly after Lady Cornwall's arrival, the house of Mistress Minthrope echoed with the sounds of a gaggle of geese mixed with a cacophony of cackles.

"Simply scandalous!" shrieked Lady Beatrice.

"Shameful!" followed Mistress Priscilla.

"I have never heard of such a thing!" snarled Lady Constance.

Mistress Carleen nasally screeched, "Courting someone of the *labouring-class?*"

"Beyond reproach!"
"Preposterous!"
"Despicable!"
"Disgraceful!"
"SCANDALOUS!"
"SCANDALOUS!"
"SCANDALOUS!"

When the news made it all the way around the room to Mistress Jezebel, she froze as though struck by a bullet. Initial shock over, she maniacally screamed, "Wretched wench! I will kill her!" She sprinted erratically to a distraught Lady Cobham, and ripped at her mother's clothing. "Mother, I want her killed! Kill the labouring-class wench! Kill her! I want her dead!"

After dinner that evening, as Samantha read books in the library, she overheard two maidservants gossiping.

"God strike me *dead* if it not be the *Gospel Truth!* Mistress Jezebel says she will 'ave

Mistress Talbot *murdered* if Baron Campbell won't court 'er!"

"But tell me *why* Mistress Jezebel wishes Mistress Talbot kilt?"

"Me and Julie 'eard Baron Campbell speak on 'is feelin's! The baron says to Sir Peter, 'Only Samantha 'as me 'eart. I wish to 'ave *no other!*'"

"But, 'ow do you know Mistress Jezebel wishes Samantha Talbot kilt?"

"Sally told me so at the market!"

"What *more* did Sally say? Tell me *more!*"

The first servant laughed mischievously and continued. "Sally tells me 'bouts 'ow every day or two, she spies a scallywag in Mistress Jezebel's bed with 'er! She says Mistress Jezebel's mother bluffs she's *unawares!*"

"Ohhhhhhh!" The servant girls giggled at high pitch catching the attention of Gertrude, who rasped, "Get your fannies in the kitchen and back to work this 'ere instant! Ignorant, gossipin' nitwits!"

Samantha heard the girls clomp and clatter quickly to the kitchen. *Could Jezebel's supposed threat be cause for concern?* she wondered.

No! She is simply a spoiled girl, overly-desirous of male companionship—and not of solely one male. She is harmless; I am sure.

Samantha's next thought brought on a contented smile—the servant's comment regarding John's feelings. *John's heart belongs to me!*

She closed her eyes, breathed a happy sigh, and returned to reading her book.

Chapter 20

One morning two weeks later, Samantha lay awake looking out of her bedchamber window. *Will we ever be able to sleep in the same bed? My body cries out for you, John!*

As though John had heard her thoughts, he entered Samantha's bedchamber. "Samantha, I need to talk to you."

Samantha sat upright with a smile. "Of course. What is it?"

John walked over to her bed, and sat down next to her. He somberly spoke, "I feel I may be doing you a disservice if I continue my courtship with you... I fear I am only hurting you."

Astonished by this sudden change, Samantha earnestly responded, "No! You are not hurting me... Am I hurting you?"

"No," John responded. "But I need to be honest. I need to let you know... I am concerned. Maybe you would live a happier life with the people of...*your* community."

"I understand," said Samantha. *No! I do not understand! These words you speak are hurting my* heart! *I cannot lose you now, John; I love you too much!*

John looked down regretfully.

Samantha felt tears bursting to come out. She tried hard to hold them in; however the emotion overwhelmed her, and the tears poured out in seeming torrents.

John pulled her close in a comforting embrace. "Do not trouble yourself," he said. "We will get through this... Somehow we will make this work..."

Samantha tried to smile, but she worried. *Maybe he only says this to quiet my tears. Maybe he plans to leave me to my labouring-class world forever. I would not blame him...*

Down the hallway, John's eleven-year-old, Sarah, awoke. "Today, we celebrate Harvest Festival at church!"

"How do you know?" inquired Samantha's eleven-year-old, Tessa.

"Because last evening, I saw the Harvest Moon! Let us dress in our Sunday best for church!"

Sarah and Tessa readied themselves, and scrambled excitedly to the other children's bedchambers to announce the holiday celebration. Soon, all sat joking and giggling at the long table downstairs in the banquet hall.

Lady Cornwall strutted pretentiously past the children wearing an outlandish gown featuring several long ostrich plumes and an overabundance of gaudy jewels. At her exit, she turned toward the children, and wrinkled her nose in disgust. She rasped, "Quiet down! This is not *circus day!* It is *Sunday*, and on *Sunday* one must maintain *SOBRIETY!*"

The children sat stunned as Lady Cornwall exited in search of Sir Peter, whom she found in the formal dining hall. "Where have the servants placed our harvest donation for the harvest charity? We must see that our contribution is *far and above* that of the MacKenzies'. I do *not* wish another year of Lady MacKenzie's *endless boasting.*"

Sir Peter matter-of-factly responded, "The wagonloads stand ahead of the carriages, full of produce and ready for church. I assure you our contribution is exemplary."

Lady Cornwall departed immediately to inspect the wagons. As Sir Peter had promised, they overflowed bountifully. However, Lady Cornwall sniffed the air discontentedly, and instructed her footman, "Help me to my carriage!"

The footman did so, and Lady Cornwall sat scowling as she awaited the others.

After breakfast, Sir Peter escorted everyone out to the carriages. He sat next to Lady Cornwall, who complained to their driver, "We are late! Our wagons were to be *first* in line!"

Although not his fault, the driver responded, "My sincerest apologies, Lady Cornwall."

Lady Cornwall said nothing. She simply displayed her disapproving visage.

Momentarily presenting a disgusted expression, Sir Peter soon appeared to dismiss his wife's rudeness as a matter of course.

John, Samantha and the children quickly settled into their carriages, and all departed. Upon their arrival at St. Edward's Church, Samantha's eyes widened. *I have never seen so much charity! The line of overflowing wagons seems endless!*

After seating themselves inside the church, Father Peterson initiated the morning worship service by thanking his parishioners for their abundant offerings.

Lady Cornwall stood up and curtseyed, as though she were the only one to whom he gave thanks.

Samantha whispered to John, "Oh my! She *is* quite full of herself, isn't she?"

John smiled and nodded in agreement.

After church, as footmen helped aristocrats into carriages, a spine-chilling scream pierced the air. It stemmed from Mistress Jezebel, who shrieked and cried uncontrollably outside of her carriage. "I *saw* her! She sat beside *him!* Oh, Mother, how it *tortures* me!"

Oh dear! Not Jezebel again, thought Samantha as she entered the carriage behind the Cobham's. *This is really quite embarrassing.*

John joined Samantha, and put his arm around her.

Jezebel witnessed this, and shrieked louder.

Lady Zelda Cobham attempted to muffle her daughter's cries by holding her head tightly to her shoulder. She signaled her footman for assistance, and they helped Jezebel into her carriage.

Lady Cornwall rushed over to join her sister and niece on the short journey to Lord Cobham's residence.

Over intermittent shrieks of hysteria, Lady Zelda Cobham shouted, "Thank you, my good sister, for repairing with me to my home! I am in dire need of your support, *and* we need to plan!"

Lady Cornwall responded, "Much better for me *not* to return to my residence! This bloody holiday will have the damnable heathens noisily frolicking, and I would *not* be able to tolerate it!"

"Must you blaspheme at this hour?" Lady Zelda Cobham sniveled. "I told you we need to plan!"

Mistress Jezebel shrieked again, and Lady Cornwall displayed a disdainful expression.

Dear Lord, what detestable people they are! Samantha snuggled close to John as the carriages departed.

Chapter 21

On the tenth of October, as the children sat at the long banquet table awaiting breakfast, Sir Peter entered the banquet hall singing, *"He who eats goose on Michaelmas Day; shan't money, lack, or debts to pay!"*

The children giggled, and John's ten-year-old William asked, "Uncle Peter, sir, is today Michaelmas Day?"

Sir Peter replied, "I saw the cooks stuffing more than one goose with apples for dinner, so what do you suspect?"

The children happily responded, "It *is* Michaelmas Day!"

"So, what more does Michaelmas Day mean, Sir Peter?" asked Samantha's sixteen-year-old, Ethan.

"A dark Michaelmas means a light Christmas... We need to check the sky!"

"And what else, Uncle Peter?" asked four-year-old Henry, smiling.

"If St. Michael brings many acorns, snow will cover the fields at Christmas... We need to check the acorns!"

"That sounds like jolly good fun!" exclaimed Tabitha, and the other children agreed.

John entered and teased, "What is all of this happy commotion about?"

Tessa answered, "Sir Peter is teaching us all about today's holiday!"

John smiled and dramatized, "Ah, yes! Today is the day the devil was kicked out of Heaven, and as he fell from the skies, he landed in a bramble bush... He cursed the fruit of that prickly plant, and scorched them with his fiery breath!"

Samantha entered interjecting, "Therefore, it is bad luck to pick blackberries until next season!"

John grabbed Samantha, and kissed her cheek. "You are correct, Sweetheart!"

He kissed her again, and some of the children cried, "Ewwwwwwww!"

"Stop kissing her!" exclaimed Rachel.

John pulled Samantha close, and put on a dramatic show of kissing her romantically. He followed with, "Well, why not kiss her? This is the lady I love!"

"Ewwwwwwww!" some of the children cried again.

John's oldest daughter, Amanda, said, "I think it is *lovely*, Father! You have my vote for continued success!"

"I agree," Tessa affirmed with smiling eyes. "I think it is lovely, too!"

He loves me? Samantha could not believe what she had heard. *Could my dream be coming true?   Is it possible?*   She stood blithely entranced.

Sir Peter stood reticently, with a stone-faced expression.

Chapter 22

"Boooooooooooooooooooooooooo!" voiced John and Sir Peter outside the childrens' bedchambers three weeks after Michaelmas Day.   They continued making ghostly noises until some of the children awoke and started screaming.

When Sarah and Tessa peered into the hallway, John grabbed them and tickled them.

One by one, as they became aware of the game, the younger children ventured out in hopes of being tickled, too.

Sir Peter watched with a contented visage.

Tabitha exclaimed, "Tonight must be All Hallows Evening—October 31st! Is that why you make ghost noises, Father?"

"Correct, Tabitha. Tonight is the night we dress as ghosts and tell ghost stories around a bonfire!"

"Hurrah!" shouted several of the children.

John suddenly turned and headed downstairs, making ghost noises until he reached the lower floor.

Sir Peter followed, grinning all the way.

Evening finally arrived, and Sir Peter boomed, "Here ye! Here ye! The hour of apple bobbing has arrived! Here ye! Here ye! Come one! Come all! To the dance hall!"

The children excitedly followed Sir Peter's orders, and took turns dunking their faces in the barrel of floating apples until successfully arising apple in mouth. Only Baby Kathryn used her hands to assist with the activity.

Next, John organized a treasure hunt for masks. He and Samantha had hidden enough ghost masks all over the lower floor for each child and servant to obtain one.

Once all the masks were found, Sir Peter announced, "The bonfire is ready!"

He provided his servants with flambeaux— flaming torches, and led the group of "ghosts" outdoors behind the mansion. Everyone marched down a trail to the bonfire, with the exception of

Lady Cornwall who remained inside with "a sick headache."

At the bonfire, Sir Peter passed a stick containing an apple at its end to each child and servant.

Samantha smiled. *I could almost accustom myself to this place!*

They roasted the apples, and one of the masked servants collected them to make a unique drink.

John announced, "My father taught me this tradition upon his return from his ancestral home in Ireland."

Everyone watched the servant as she crushed the roasted apples and mixed them with cream, sugar, and spices in a large iron pot. Afterwards, she distributed pieces of toast to everyone, and John said, "Tear up your toast, and throw the pieces into the pot."

After doing so, the children shouted, "They float!"

John explained, "The clumps of floating toast give this drink its name."

"Lambs-wool!" exclaimed Amanda proudly.

143

"Correct!" John acknowledged. "We call this drink *lambs-wool*."

"The bread *does* look like lambs' wool," commented Ethan.

The servant placed a ladle inside the pot, and all took turns sipping from it.

Samantha observed the various expressions the children made upon tasting the traditional Irish drink. *Quite amusing!* She giggled.

Next, John instructed, "Bring forth the bowls of callcannon!"

Callcannon? What next? Samantha grinned contentedly as masked servants placed bowl after bowl on a table next to John. He wore a giant black cape, which he spread over the table by flinging his arms out to his sides. Using a mysterious voice, he pretended to cast a magic spell on the bowls.

Facing everyone, he explained, "Callcannon is another Irish tradition! Before you take a bite of this mixture of potatoes, parsnips and onions; you must know that one of these bowls contains a ring."

"Ooooooooooh!" marveled several of the girls.

John continued, "And as the tradition goes, the one who finds the ring in his or her bowl will be married before next Hallows Eve'!"

"May we begin?" squealed Sarah.

"You may begin!" replied John.

The girls scraped and scraped enthusiastically at their bowls, all coming up empty.

The boys ate their callcannon hungrily, and voiced relief at not having found a ring in their bowls.

All eyes looked around to see where the ring ended up.

Suddenly, Samantha smiled brightly and inquired, "John?" *Could this be a marriage proposal?*

John winked at her, and walked over to kiss her forehead. "Unfortunately, I cannot promise anything at this time. There are many things to consider..."

"Of course," said Samantha, careful not to display her disappointment.

She placed the ring on her right ring finger. "How amazingly exotic! *Thank you!*"

John spoke quietly, "You are most welcome, Sweetheart."

"What type of stone is it?" inquired Samantha.

"It is a pearl from French Polynesia of the South Seas. I purchased it from an oriental peddler."

Samantha's eyes sparkled happily as the girls gathered round to admire her new, silvery-blackish, peacock-greenish pearl ring.

Adam interrupted them. "May we begin with the ghost stories?"

Sir Peter's expression shifted from appalled to childishly giddy, and he announced, "Yes! Let us do!"

All attention turned towards him.

He held up a hollowed turnip, carved with a ghoulish face. Fire flickered from within. "I introduce to you Jack-of-the-Lantern! Come close, so that I may tell you his story!"

Everyone gathered round Sir Peter, and he continued. "Jack-of-the-Lantern was a man formerly known as Stingy Jack... Stingy Jack was *so mean and stingy* that when he finally died, St. Peter refused to allow him into Heaven. Moreover, since he had played too many tricks on the Devil; the Devil refused his entry into Hell! So, Stingy

Jack was forced to spend the rest of eternity on earth, where he nightly carries a carved turnip lantern with a burning coal inside... And, that, my dear ones, is how Stingy Jack became known as Jack O'Lantern!"

Rachel trembled. "Uncle Peter, sir, your Jack O'Lantern frightens me! Maybe it will bring Stingy Jack to *us!*"

John spoke to his young daughter, "No need to fear, Rachel. The bonfire will scare off all evil ghosts and goblins—including Stingy Jack!"

Sir Peter added, "In fact, that is why we celebrate All Hallows Eve' with a bonfire—to scare them away for a full year."

Rachel appeared relieved.

William asked, "What about the Grim Reaper? Will the bonfire keep the Grim Reaper away for a full year?"

John and Sir Peter looked at each other, and Sir Peter deferred to John.

"The Grim Reaper is different. If I knew a sure way to keep him away forever and always, I would certainly follow through with whatever it took."

Those with their masks off peered with wide eyes into the shadows as if the Grim Reaper stood nearby.

Adam worsened things by adding, "I have heard tell the Grim Reaper especially takes pleasure in visiting during the *dark, winter* months."

William made an evil, gutteral sound.

Some of the children screamed.

Samantha calmed them with, "We are all of good health. Do not trouble yourselves!"

Sir Peter interjected, "Let us drink to that! I have reserved some of my finest wine for this All Hallows Eve'—Sauvignon Blanc!"

While servants distributed goblets of the white wine, Samantha stood mesmerized by her ring.

"Wine, madam?" a masked servant asked.

Samantha did not respond.

"Madam?   Mistress Talbot?"

"Why yes, I would love some!" she finally enthused, grasping the silver goblet.

Turning to John, she clinked his goblet, saying, "To good health!"

"To good health, my love."

John turned to Ethan, clinked his goblet, reiterating Samantha's toast; and the toast went likewise around the bonfire.

After gulping down his wine, William feigned shock and fear. "By King George, I see the Grim Reaper!"

Rachel screamed, and ran to Samantha for safety. As she grabbed hold of her legs, Samantha collapsed and fell to the ground.

"The Grim Reaper killed Samantha!" yelled Rachel. "Help! Father!"

Kneeling over Samantha, John lifted her head, and witnessed a stream of blood draining from her mouth. He scooped her up in an instant, and carried her swiftly to the mansion where he set her down on her favorite chaise longue in the library.

Shaking her gently, he called, "Samantha, wake up! Wake up!"

Samantha's eyes opened slightly. Her face glowed with perspiration. With a debilitated tone, she spoke, "Please bring me a basin. I fear I have need of vomiting."

John looked intently at a nearby maidservant who understood, and rushed off.

When the basin arrived, Samantha put it to its intended purpose and fell asleep.

Throughout the night, Samantha awoke several times—perspiring, convulsing, vomiting, and slipping back into a fitful sleep.

John remained by her side the whole while.

Chapter 23

The weather turned bitter cold, with many days of sleet and snow flurries; but all kept happy, cozy, and comfy huddling together with warm blankets in front of the various fireplaces inside Sir Peter's Gothic mansion.

Fully recovered from her Halloween ordeal, Samantha headed towards the dance hall the morning of December 21st.

John stepped into her path, and put his arm around her waist. He guided her into the conservatory. "Good morrow, Beautiful," he whispered, staring down into her shining eyes.

"Good morrow, Handsome." Samantha smiled, and reached her arms around his neck.

They kissed romantically for a long while.

Suddenly Samantha worried. "The children will be getting unruly..."

"Let us see to them together!" John grabbed Samantha's hand, and pulled her towards the dance hall.

As they peered inside, Sarah announced, "Today is St. Thomas Day...the beginning of Christmas!"

Tessa asked, "What does your family do for St. Thomas Day?"

"This is the day we begin Christmas caroling in the evening. We stand in front of our neighbors' houses and sing Christmas songs!"

Samantha entered the dance hall followed by John. "I once heard that my favorite saint—St. Francis of Assisi—was the *first* to develop Christmas carols, sung at church way back in the 1200s. He changed the lyrics of well-known songs to religious lyrics, so that his congregation could learn about the Bible."

John added, "And when Oliver Cromwell took control of England in the 1600s, he banned Christmas carols from churches, so *outdoor* caroling began."

Samantha asked, "How about we practice some Christmas carols now?"

The children responded affirmatively, and Samantha led them in singing "Deck the Halls."

While they sang, everyone heard the scurrying back and forth of servants in the entrance hall.

"The servants are decorating!" shouted Tabitha excitedly. "They are decorating the halls for Christmas!"

Everyone continued singing, *"See the blazing Yule before us...fa la la la la..."*

When they finished the song, Uncle Peter stepped into the dance hall, and William asked, "Uncle Peter, may we hunt for a Yule log today?"

"That sounds like a magnificent plan, William. If Mistress Talbot does not mind, we could postpone today's lesson, and hunt for one directly."

Samantha enthused, "It would be my pleasure!"

The children happily hurried to bundle up in their winter outer-clothing, and search for the largest log they could find. Sir Peter, Samantha, and John joined them to observe the fun.

As expected, the two oldest boys retrieved the largest logs. They placed them before Sir Peter, inquiring, "Which is the biggest?" and "Whose gets to be the Yule log?"

Sir Peter, John, and Samantha agreed that both logs, although completely different in shape, were about equal.

Sir Peter announced, "We have *two* winners! For the twelve days of Christmas, Ethan's will light the *dance hall* whilst Adam's will light the *banquet hall!*"

Nobody argued over this solution, and Sir Peter appeared quite proud of his diplomacy.

John whispered to Samantha, "I think I see some mistletoe."

"Where?"

"Come with me. I will show you."

Samantha followed John into a clump of trees. She giggled, asking, "Where is it?"

When fully secluded, he embraced her and kissed her passionately.

After their kiss, Samantha smiled at John. "There is no mistletoe over here!"

John laughed and winked. "Did there need to be?"

"No!" Samantha laughed, and pulled John close to kiss him in return.

Following tradition, all of the children took turns dragging the Yule logs back to the mansion. They believed the superstition that taking part in this endeavor would bring them luck for an entire year.

Inside the mansion, Sir Peter placed Ethan's log into the dance hall fireplace, and gave the following Yule blessing:

> Bless thee, Yule;
>> Light the winter sky;
> Bless thee Yule;
>> Bake the mincemeat pie;

Bless thee Yule;
       Bring us silent nights;
Bless thee Yule;
       Give us seldom fights.

Finally, Sir Peter poured some wine onto the Yule log, and everyone applauded.

What a strange custom. Samantha stared quizzically at Sir Peter. *It seems sacrilegious!*

Sir Peter repeated the ceremony in the banquet hall with Adam's Yule log, and Samantha said to the children, "That was all in good fun; but we know that only God can provide us with the things, about which Sir Peter spoke."

Sir Peter assented, "Mistress Talbot is correct. This was *only* in the spirit of good fun."

Later, when the darkness of a winter evening blanketed the mansion, Henry and Rachel burst inside the front door. "The carolers are coming!"

All of the mansion's inhabitants—even Lady Cornwall—filled windows and doorways at the front of Sir Peter's mansion to watch while several of their neighbors stood bunched together outside holding torches and singing carols with the genuine enthusiasm and spirit of Christmas. After almost fifteen minutes, the carolers turned to walk to the next estate.

Tessa and Sarah ran to Samantha and John. "May we join the carolers, or start our own caroling group?"

Samantha looked to John, who replied, "Let us plan that for the morrow, shall we?"

"Thank you, Baron Campbell!" exclaimed Tessa.

"Yes, thank you, Father!" followed Sarah, hugging him.

After tucking the children into bed, John found Samantha in the hallway. He pushed her gently into her bedchamber and against a wall. Pressing his firm manhood against her, he gave her a warm, loving kiss.

"Father!" cried little Henry from his bedchamber down the hallway. "Father!"

Damn! thought Samantha.

John gave Samantha a pained expression. "I had better go to him."

"Of course," Samantha agreed.

Looking deeply into her eyes, John said, "I love you, Sweetheart. Sweet dreams."

"I love you, too, Handsome." Samantha gazed at John as he left her chamber to care for his son. *We were so close!*

She dressed in her nightgown, brushed her hair, and climbed into bed. *Alone again...*

Suddenly, Samantha sat upright. *He told me he loves me!* She sighed contentedly, and lay back down with a huge smile on her face.

Chapter 24

John kept his promise, and took the children caroling the evenings of December 22nd and 23rd. Samantha and Sir Peter joined them, and all had fun.

On Christmas Eve morning, Samantha awoke and lay contemplating a mysterious feeling. *Death lurks nearby...*

Interrupting her, the children marched past her chamber singing Christmas carols. Amanda had awoken first; and with the help of Sarah and Tessa, she rushed around to the other children queuing them up for an indoor caroling session.

Samantha threw on her robe to follow along.

Passing John's bedchamber, he stepped out and put his hands around her waist forming the tail end of the queue.

Samantha looked back at John, who grinned and whispered, "Good morrow, Love."

"Good morrow," Samantha whispered in return. *Handsome as always. You melt my heart, John!*

Passing Lady Cornwall's bedchamber, Gertrude stepped out and sharply reprimanded, "Quiet down. M'Lady Sue still sleeps, and she must 'aves 'er beauty sleep!"

The children sang more softly as Amanda led them to the banquet hall for breakfast.

161

Maidservants brought in eggs, bacon, and freshly baked bread while the happy children chorused:

> Good tidings we bring,
> To you and your kin,
> Good tidings for Christmas,
> And a happy new year.
>
> Now bring us some figgy pudding,
> Now bring us some figgy pudding,
> Now bring us some figgy pudding,
> And a cup of good cheer.
>
> We won't go until we get some!
> We won't go until we get some!
> We won't go until we get some!
> So bring some out here!

Elsabelle, one of the kitchen servants, fretfully responded, "We don't got no figgy puddin' this 'ere mornin', but we'll get to workin' on it fer the morrow."

As she started for the kitchen, John said, "That will be fine, Elsabelle. The children and I will *appreciate* that." He gestured to the children, so they would use their manners.

"Thank you, Elsabelle! Merry Christmas, Elsabelle!" the children exclaimed.

Elsabelle bowed her head and completed her exit, while John grinned and winked approvingly at the children.

Sir Peter entered next, happily descanting, "Merry Christmas to one and all! Take care to fill your stomachs *not too much,* for I have set the servants to preparing an afternoon feast fit for King George and all of his men!"

"Sounds wonderful!" exclaimed Samantha. The children beamed at one another and Sir Peter.

During the afternoon, while a torrential winter rain fell outside, the inhabitants of the Gothic mansion enjoyed a bountiful Christmas feast with all the trimmings Sir Peter had promised.

Later, after returning from the midnight worship service at church and tucking the children into bed, Samantha stood in the upstairs hallway inhaling contentedly. *How magnificent! Warm, cozy, and safe inside.* She closed her eyes, and bowed her head to pray. *Thank you, Lord, for the blessings of this Christmas...*

Before she could finish her prayer, John walked up behind her and pulled her close.

Samantha smiled and swiveled to face him. "Merry Christmas, my love!" she exclaimed softly.

"Merry Christmas to you."

Samantha reached her arms around John's neck, and they shared a romantic Christmas kiss.

"Good night, my beloved," John whispered.

"Good night, Handsome." Samantha gazed admiringly at John, and he turned to walk to his bedchamber. *Maybe by next Christmas, you will have no need of walking away!* Her nether region throbbed desirously.

Her next thought made her gasp. *He called me "beloved"!* Samantha smiled, and headed for her bed.

Chapter 25

Shortly after dawn of Christmas morning, before the children could taste their figgy pudding, Samantha could hear someone running all over the mansion. *Who might that be?* Already dressed, she walked downstairs.

Upon reaching the bottom step, Sir Peter's footman ran to her frantically voicing, "Sir Peter! Where is 'e?"

Before she could respond, John stepped out of the conservatory, asking, "What is it, Reginald? Is there a problem?"

"Baron Campbell! Lord Cobham is 'ere! In the entrance! 'is cheeks...all stained with tears! Can't find Sir Peter! Can't find 'im nowheres!"

Calm and deliberate, John said, "I will see to Lord Cobham."

Samantha followed John to the edge of the entrance hall, where she caught sight of Lord Cobham standing near the front door. She stopped at this point to allow John to speak with the lord privately. *He does appear distraught!*

After Lord Cobham left, John firmly instructed several nearby maidservants, "Find Sir

Peter. It is imperative I speak with him. Direct him to the 'drawing room."

Not wishing to interfere, Samantha simply followed John as he swiftly walked to the kitchen. Upon finding Gertrude, he urgently spoke, "Lady Cornwall is to be dressed immediately, and directed to the 'drawing room. Assist her at once!"

A short while later, Gertrude and Lady Cornwall entered the withdrawing room.

John spoke gravely, "Susan, I need you to sit down on the sofa. I have terrible news to report to you."

Lady Cornwall sat down slowly, asking, "What terrible news?"

"It is in regards to your sister," John began. "Lord Cobham was here... I regretfully must inform you that your sister has been found...dead."

"No!" exclaimed Lady Cornwall. Rising, she screamed erratically, "You are lying! No! I will not believe you!"

Turning to Gertrude, she voiced, "Where is Peter? Get Peter!"

As Gertrude exited in search of Sir Peter, Lady Cornwall flailed her arms, and slapped John several times in the face and on top of his head screaming, "Liar!"

Dear God! She goes crazy! Samantha felt helpless.

John grabbed both of Lady Cornwall's arms, and called out, "Samantha, get the male servants—out in the barn!"

Grateful for John's guidance, Samantha hurried out. *What could have happened to Lady Zelda Cobham?*

She quickly returned with two male servants, who subdued Lady Cornwall.

The maidservants sent earlier to retrieve Sir Peter entered the room, and the first whined, "Baron Campbell, sir, we looked *everywheres*, and Sir Peter is *nowheres!*"

John turned to them. "I think I know where he is. Everyone is to remain here whilst Samantha and I search for him."

He grabbed Samantha's hand, and they exited the withdrawing room. Leading her to the gallery, John entered and walked over to the monstrous painting of King George III on the rear wall. He peered around the edge of the wooden frame—first on the left side; then on the right.

He nodded his head. "Exactly as I thought!" Glancing behind him, he said, "See that we have no witnesses!"

Samantha surveyed the entrance hall and vicinity. Approaching John, she assured, "All clear."

John pushed the frame on the right side of the painting, causing the whole section of wall behind it to revolve. He looked at Samantha.

She gazed at him, starry-eyed and awestruck. *You impress me, John!*

He winked, grabbed her hand, and they entered the secret doorway.

Descending a stairwell, they could hear low groans.

Halfway down, John whispered, "Wait for me here, Love." He continued his descent to the servant floor.

Peering around the corner of the stairwell, he could see Sir Peter. He sat on a bed with breeches pushed down to his ankles; eyes closed; face upward. A pretty, redheaded servant with pitted complexion and a deep scar on her right cheek performed fellatio as Sir Peter grunted pleasurably.

Unsure how to halt the action, John caught sight of the woman's skillful hands stroking Sir Peter's manhood while she expertly used her mouth, lips, and tongue in a way John had never seen before—in a way he wished Samantha could perform.

He returned to the stairwell, and whispered, "Be sure to remain here."

"Why?"

"I will explain *fully* at a later date," John assured. He returned to the servant floor.

As the woman stood up attempting to remove her dress, John said, "Peter!"

Sir Peter scrambled to cover himself, while his voice reverberated at an uneven pitch. "*Good God, man!* What on *God's good earth* are you doing here?"

John earnestly stated, "Your presence is required upstairs in the 'drawing room. You will understand the urgency once you ascend."

John bowed to the redheaded woman, and headed upstairs with Samantha.

★

A short while later, Sir Peter reached the main floor where the sound of a woman's wailing greeted him. Entering the withdrawing room, he discovered the source of the commotion—his wife, Lady Cornwall.

"You are all liars!" she screamed. "She is *not* dead!"

The male servants loosened their grip on Lady Cornwall, and she ran to Sir Peter. She clawed at his clothing, and moaned, "Tell them they are all liars, Peter!"

"Who is dead?" Sir Peter inquired, "What ill befalls us? Someone explain!"

John began, "Your wife's sister...Zelda Cobham..."

Lady Cornwall interjected, "No! He is lying, Peter! Make him leave!"

John continued, "Lord Cobham informed us her body was discovered only an hour ago. I will explain the particulars to you when..."

"Bring her some brandywine!" Sir Peter interjected, glaring at one of his male servants.

The stunned servant froze, and Sir Peter bellowed, "This instant!"

The servant fled the room, and hastily returned with a goblet of brandywine.

Lady Cornwall gulped the contents in its entirety, and lay down on a sofa with a despondent expression.

Sir Peter dismissed John, saying, "I will take watch of her now."

Everyone wasted no time in vacating the withdrawing room—with the exception of Gertrude, who sat down beside Lady Cornwall to massage her lady's temples.

Later, as the children played quietly in the game room, Samantha spoke softly to John in the library. "It was eery, John... I awakened yesterday with a strange feeling that Death lurked nearby. Then, within twenty-four hours, we learn Lady Zelda Cobham is found dead!"

Remaining silent, John reached out to pull Samantha close for a loving embrace.

"How do you suppose she died?" Samantha asked.

"I only wish I knew, Samantha." He kissed her forehead.

Back in the withdrawing room, Sir Peter and Gertrude tranquilized and comforted Lady Cornwall the remainder of Christmas Day. At nighttime, John and Samantha went to check on them.

"Is there anything we can do?" John asked his brother.

"No... Thank you." Turning to Gertrude, Sir Peter instructed, "I think it is time we retire. Let us carry Lady Cornwall to her bedchamber. We will assist her more efficiently after a night's slumber."

They carried Lady Cornwall's limp and cumbersome body to her bed, and laid her down. Sir Peter walked to the doorway, where John and

Samantha peered in. Turning back, he said, "Come along, Gertrude."

Gertrude stared at him with pleading eyes. She gutterally voiced, "I needs to stay with 'er. I needs to nurse 'er, m'lord."

Sounding exhausted, Sir Peter acquiesced. "As you please." He about-faced, and all exited for their bedchambers.

Chapter 26

Early the following morning, John and Sir Peter saddled up horses, and headed for Lord Cobham's to learn more about Lady Zelda Cobham's death. When they arrived, a servant rushed over to retrieve their horses while another escorted them to Lord Cobham's study. There, the forlorn widower sat with a dazed expression.

"Tell us exactly what transpired," Sir Peter spoke compassionately.

Lord Cobham looked up, bowed his head to acknowledge their presence, and slowly spoke. "One of my servants found her face down, lying prostrate in a puddle only a short distance from the house. When he turned her over, blood flowed from her mouth. She was already dead."

"Excuse me, m'lord," interjected a servant. "The town coroner is here to see you."

"Send him in," instructed Lord Cobham.

"Good morrow, gentlemen." The coroner entered Lord Cobham's study. Turning to John, he said, "The name's Shane Keaney."

John shook his hand.

"I have come to report my preliminary findings."

"Please," encouraged Lord Cobham.

"I have found the *primary* cause of Lady Cobham's death to be drowning. However, the *initial* cause was...poisoning."

The gentlemen appeared stupefied.

"Clarify this for me," pleaded the bereft widower.

"I believe your wife, sir, was *initially* poisoned; she *subsequently* collapsed face first into the rain puddle; which *ultimately* caused her to drown."

"Was my wife murdered?" Lord Cobham inquired. His face had lost all color, and he trembled slightly.

Mister Keaney replied, "I am not disposed to make any conclusive judgment regarding murder at this point. Do you know of anyone who would want to poison your wife?"

The widower responded, "I have no earthly idea. She has always been a charitable person. She has been well-liked by most everyone in the community... I am utterly perplexed."

After a moment of silence, John said to Lord Cobham, "Whoever may have wanted your wife murdered, may have also poisoned Samantha."

Everyone drew in a breath, and John explained. "On All Hallows Eve', my Samantha collapsed after drinking white wine from a goblet. As she lay unconscious, blood drained from her mouth..."

After briefly contemplating John's words, Mister Keaney said, "Thank you, Baron Campbell. I will study this further. I must confer with Mister Johannes."

John presented a quizzical expression, and Mister Keaney clarified. "Erick Johannes, Stow's apothecary, is working on Lady Cobham's blood to verify the poisoning agent for me. I will keep you abreast of whatever we may come to ascertain."

Sir Peter reached out to shake Mister Keaney's hand. "Thank you, my good man. You have been most diligent. We would appreciate all you could do to assist us with our unanswered questions." He handed the coroner a large bag filled with money.

Mister Keaney bowed his head thankfully, and departed.

Chapter 27

The next day, John and Sir Peter sat with Lord Cobham under his front portico waiting for the coroner, Keaney, to return.

By late afternoon, he rode up on his horse. "Good afternoon, gentlemen!"

"Good afternoon, Mister Keaney!" John responded. "Have you come bearing conclusive information?"

"Yes sir, Baron, I have," replied Mister Keaney, dismounting and stepping onto the portico.

In a more somber tone, Mister Keaney spoke, "It is as I had suspected. Lady Zelda Cobham, *your wife* Lord Cobham, was poisoned by arsenic—common rat poison..."

"Moreover," he continued, "Mister Johannes informed me that he records all purchases made at his shop. His books show October and December purchases of arsenic by the Cobham household; however, he found no record of arsenic purchased during the past five years by the Cornwall residence, where Mistress Talbot was poisoned."

John inquired, "Do Mr. Johannes's records show the *name* of the person, who purchased the arsenic?"

"No," Mister Keaney replied. "He says he records the households based on the color of livery the servants wear. In other words, the servant who purchased the arsenic during the months of October and December wore the violet livery of Lord Cobham's household; whereas there is no record, within the past five years, of any arsenic purchased by a servant wearing the dark blue livery of Sir Peter's."

Later that evening, Samantha softly knocked on Lady Cornwall's bedchamber door. When no one answered, she opened the door to find Lady Cornwall and Gertrude in bed together—without a trace of clothing. Gertrude's left hand caressed one of Lady Cornwall's bare breasts.

"Oh dear...excuse me!" exclaimed Samantha. *I always knew there was something different about their relationship...*

Lady Cornwall opened her eyes and demanded, "What are you doing in here?"

"Sir Peter informed me that y-you have had trouble sleeping... I-I brought you a tranquilizing tincture to assist you..."

"Set the tray over there!" instructed Lady Cornwall, gesturing toward her bedside table.

Samantha followed the instruction, and headed for the door.

"Bring me the tincture!" rasped Lady Cornwall.

Samantha turned back, and realized that Lady Cornwall now instructed Gertrude. She completed her exit, closing the door quietly.

Heading upstairs, Samantha met John, who headed downstairs. "John, I must speak with you," she whispered urgently.

"Come with me to the conservatory." He grabbed her hand, and led her over there.

Inside the conservatory, Samantha related what she had witnessed.

"It makes perfect sense to me, darling," John said. "I had begun to wonder if Lady Cornwall had no inner yearnings whatsoever."

Samantha appeared confused.

John smiled. "Let me explain..."

Suddenly, Samantha heard a strange murmuring sound. "What was that?"

"I heard nothing."

The murmur sounded again, and John said, "Let us find the source."

Samantha followed him as he headed toward the kitchen.

On the way, the muffled cries grew louder. They searched for the origin, and discovered that the crying stemmed from Lady Cornwall's bedchamber.

Peering inside, they saw Gertrude rocking the tranquilized and unconscious Lady Cornwall. She sobbed, "I only wished to 'ave you all to meself, m'Lady Sue. I didn't wish to 'urt *nobody*. I lost me 'ead; that's all."

John and Samantha looked knowingly at each other. They waited several minutes, and heard nothing more. They realized they had heard plenty—enough to accuse Gertrude as either the main suspect, or at least as an accomplice in the murder of Lady Cobham.

John led Samantha upstairs to her chamber. "I will inform Peter and question Gertrude in the morning. Good night, darling." He kissed her cheek, and walked to his bedchamber.

Samantha watched John step into his chamber. *When will we sleep together at night? I grow impatient, my love!*

Chapter 28

First thing the next morning, John informed Sir Peter about Gertrude. They questioned her, and she refused to confess.

Sir Peter spoke privately. "We must inform Sheriff Wallace directly."

They drove an equipage swiftly to Stow-on-the-Wold's town sheriff, Edgar Wallace, to explain what they knew.

"A council must be assembled," advised Sheriff Wallace.

"You are welcome to hold the meeting in my gallery," offered Sir Peter.

"Much obliged." Sheriff Wallace nodded gratefully.

By late afternoon, the following gentlemen assembled in Sir Peter's gallery: John, Lord Cobham, Sir Peter, the coroner Keaney, the apothecary Johannes, with Sheriff Wallace presiding.

Before the meeting, John found Samantha in the library. "We will avenge Zelda Cobham's murder *as well as* the poisoning you suffered. You will see."

Samantha pulled John close and kissed his cheek. "Thank you, John." She stared into his eyes. *You have no idea how much I love you, my avenging hero!*

Sir Peter brought Gertrude into the gallery to stand before the council while most of the inhabitants of his residence congregated in the entrance hall struggling to look and listen.

Sheriff Wallace began, "Gertrude, what do you know of the death of Lady Zelda Cobham?"

"I know nothin', sir." She stared down at the floor.

Like bloody Hell, you don't! Samantha's eyes gaped incredulously.

Sheriff Wallace continued, "Have you had at any time in your possession the rat poison known as arsenic?"

"No, sir."

John sharply interjected, "Have you ever used arsenic to kill rats?"

188

"No." Gertrude's voice quavered. "I don't know nothin' 'bout no rat poison."

John commanded, "Look at us when you speak!"

Gertrude kept her eyes lowered.

"Look at us, *damn you!*" Sir Peter yelled.

In the entrance hall, Samantha looked over at Lady Cornwall, who stood nearby trembling.

"Look at us!" reiterated Mr. Keaney.

"I can't!"

"Why not?" croaked Lord Cobham.

The room quieted, all awaiting her response.

Suddenly, Gertrude maniacally screamed, "I needs m'Lady Sue! I *needs* 'er!" She wailed and writhed with the countenance of a veritable lunatic. She tried to run, but John tackled and pinned her to the ground before she made it three feet.

He lifted her up, and held her in place. "Get me some rope!"

"I will get the rope!" yelled Samantha, running for the back door.

Gertrude tried her best to release herself from John's grip, but he held her firmly.

189

Samantha soon returned with the requested rope and two male servants.

The servants held Gertrude down while John tied her to a chair.

Once secured, Sheriff Wallace shouted at Gertrude, "Tell us what transpired with Lady Cobham!"

Gertrude did not respond. She closed her eyes, and tucked her head to her chest.

"Tell us, or we'll bring in Lady Cornwall!" threatened Sheriff Wallace.

Lady Cornwall gasped. She stared fearfully at Gertrude.

Gertrude raised her head; and with squinting eyes, looked out into the entrance hall. Scanning the gathered crowd, she spotted Lady Cornwall and sat up straight. "'Twas Sally! 'Twas Sally kilt Lady Cobham!" she blurted.

The gentlemen looked at each other, and nodded. It made sense since they knew the arsenic had been purchased by someone wearing the Cobham violet livery.

"Why did Sally do it?" growled Lord Cobham.

Speaking with a child's voice, Gertrude whined, "I needs m'Lady Sue." She looked over at Lady Cornwall, who appeared flabbergasted.

"How do you know Sally did it?" inquired Sheriff Wallace brusquely.

"M'Lady Sue! She's all I 'ave!" Gertrude reiterated again and again with a dazed expression.

How tragic! thought Samantha. *What a tormented life this woman must lead!*

Sheriff Wallace looked at the other gentlemen of the council and said, "Let us retrieve Sally."

Sir Peter ordered his male servants to stand guard over Gertrude, while he and the other council members headed for the Cobham residence.

About an hour later, the council members reassembled at Sir Peter's—this time with Lord Cobham's maidservant Sally. With the help of the male servants, Sheriff Wallace tied her to a chair next to Gertrude. He resumed the trial, directing his inquiry to Sally. "Gertrude here claims you are guilty of poisoning Lady Zelda Cobham, leading to her death. How do you plead?"

Appearing petrified, Sally surveyed the council members with bulging eyes. She turned to her side, gawked at Gertrude, and squealed, "Gertrude made me do it!"

Gertrude sat with a blank expression, unaffected by the accusation.

"Why?" Sheriff Wallace sharply asked.

Sally blubbered, "She told me if I didn't poison Lady Cobham, she would tell what we does when we meets on the path to the market... 'Bouts 'ow we is sometimes...*lovers!*"

The gentlemen looked at each other quizzically, and then towards Sally.

Sheriff Wallace barked, "Whatever you and Gertrude did could not possibly have been as bad as murdering someone, could it?"

"No, sir," Sally cried.

Sheriff Wallace straightened himself and calmly said to the council members, "Gentlemen, it seems time we close this trial... All in favor say 'aye'."

"Nay!" John exclaimed.

To Sally he inquired, "Why did you poison Mistress Talbot?"

"I don't know nothin' 'bout poisonin' Mistress Talbot." Appearing innocent, she added, "Honest to God in 'eaven!"

The council and crowd fell silent.

After the pause, Sheriff Wallace instructed, "Sir Peter, take me to Gertrude's bedchamber!"

Sir Peter led the council through the audience in the entrance hall downstairs to the servant floor. The sheriff searched Gertrude's chamber while the other council members looked on.

From under Gertrude's bed, Sheriff Wallace pulled out a clay jar. He opened it; and upon discovering a mysterious powder, he held it before Mister Johannes. "Can you identify this for me?"

Mister Johannes smelled it, and paused. He nodded and affirmed, "It is indeed arsenic!"

Sheriff Wallace said, "Gentlemen, these women are guilty. The trial is closed."

The council members returned to the gallery, where Sheriff Wallace formally proclaimed the guilt of the two women.

"What will be done with them?" Lord Cobham asked Sheriff Wallace.

"I will hold them at the Stow-on-the-Wold jail until I may confer with the law in London. I assure you, justice will be served!"

Lord Cobham appeared relieved as the council and audience broke with loud chatter and movement.

Thank you, dear God, prayed Samantha, *for allowing the capture of these wayward servants... May they learn the lessons their souls must learn, and cause no one to suffer again.*

She walked to John, and gave him a warm and grateful hug.

Chapter 29

A few days later, Sheriff Wallace stopped by Sir Peter's residence, and a servant showed him into the gallery.

"Greetings, sheriff!" voiced Sir Peter. "What tidings bring you here this day?"

John interjected, "What became of the servant women?"

Sheriff Wallace seated himself. "Lord Cobham's servant, Sally, now resides in the London prison." The sheriff snorted a pinch of snuff. "Whilst your servant, Gertrude, sits in a viewing cage at Bedlam."

"Bedlam?" John inquired.

Sheriff Wallace explained, "Yes, Bedlam— London's Bethlehem psychiatric hospital, an insane asylum. The lunatics are placed on display for passers-by to stop and watch—as one does with circus animals... Meanwhile, there has been a new development."

John and Sir Peter expressed interest.

"Lord Cobham informed me yesterday that his own daughter, Jezebel, confessed to putting Gertrude up to the poisoning of Mistress Talbot.

"Dear God!" exclaimed Sir Peter.

"Yes." Sheriff Wallace adjusted himself in his seat. "It seems Jezebel desired Mistress Talbot permanently removed. She thought this way she would have you for herself, Baron Campbell."

Stunned, John inquired, "What is being done about Jezebel?"

"Lord Cobham requested she be sent to a workhouse... He has no desire to see her ever again... Presently she journeys toward a most bleak affair, far removed from here..."

John commented gravely, "Justice has been served."

Sir Peter and Sheriff Wallace nodded their assent.

Chapter 30

Lady Zelda Cobham's funeral was held the twelfth day of Christmas, January 5, 1769. After the funeral, John and Sir Peter walked from the burial grounds to their carriages.

"I must inform you," began John. "I plan to return with the children and Samantha to my estate at Painswick."

Sir Peter slowed his walk. "This does not surprise me, my good brother. My abode does not hold as much...*charm* as it held previous to recent events."

John halted. "No, Peter."

Sir Peter stopped walking. Facing John, he raised an eyebrow. "No?"

John spoke earnestly. "That is not the reason. I merely think it is time we remove ourselves before overstaying our welcome... I am sure Susan could use the peace and quiet."

"Understood." Sir Peter nodded cordially, and continued walking.

Suddenly, Sir Peter's face reddened. He reached out his hand to stop John. "I have been meaning to ask you..."

"Yes?"

"Early on Christmas Day... How did you know where to find me?"

John chuckled. "You mean downstairs with the pretty redhead?"

Sir Peter nodded, and presented a slight smile.

"I had often noted the gleam in your eyes as you oftentimes focused on the painting of King George III," John explained. "Had I not known you better, I would have thought your gaze to be of a homosexual nature. However, knowing your background as I do... It became exceedingly obvious."

They grinned at each other, and walked to their respective carriages.

Late that evening, John found Samantha alone in the library. Standing before her, he inquired, "How would you feel about returning to my estate?"

"With you and the children?" Samantha enthused.

"Yes, with me and the children." He smiled.

"I would feel magnificent!" She beamed. *Thank you, God!!!!!*

"I had rather hoped you would," John flirted. He sat down next to her on the chaise longue.

"When?" inquired Samantha.

"Would tomorrow be too soon?"

Samantha gasped. "How wonderful!"

"*You're* wonderful," John said.

Samantha threw her arms around his neck. She squeezed him tightly, and pressed her cheek against his. Grabbing his head, she kissed his forehead, his ears, his neck, and began kissing her way down his chest.

All at once, they heard giggles. Looking over at the entrance hall, John and Samantha watched two young maidservants shuffle away. They smiled at each other, and John whispered lovingly, "I cannot wait to get you home!"

You have no idea how fantastic that sounds! Samantha smiled, and stared into John's eyes. "I cannot agree more!"

They stood up, and Samantha reached her arms around John's waist. She pulled him close, pressing her torso against his.

John inhaled, and closed his eyes. He lifted Samantha's chin with one finger, and kissed her one last time before returning to Painswick. "Good night, Beautiful."

"Good night, Handsome."

John headed toward his bedchamber, and Samantha lay back on the chaise longue. *Life is purely miraculous at times!*

She sighed happily, and closed her eyes.

Chapter 31

The servants packed the carriages, which stood ready for departure by the time everyone finished breakfast the next morning.

John, Samantha, and the children stepped outside the front door of the Gothic mansion. *I cannot believe this day has finally arrived! I was beginning to think it never would!* Samantha happily inhaled the fresh and cool winter air. Looking back at the mansion, she saw Sir Peter and Lady Cornwall standing in the doorway.

The children also saw them, and ran towards them shouting, "We will miss you! Thank you for having us!"

Surprisingly, each of the children embraced both Sir Peter and Lady Cornwall. At first, Lady Cornwall stood stiff as a statue. But tears filled her eyes, and she bent down to hug each child.

John hugged Sir Peter, and kissed Lady Cornwall's hand.

Samantha approached them next. She curtseyed, and bowed her head respectfully. "My sincerest gratitude for your enduring hospitality and patience."

"'Twas our utmost pleasure." Sir Peter bowed his head in return.

Lady Cornwall closed her eyes, bowing her head, also.

John, Samantha, and the children walked to their carriages. After all had entered, John signaled the drivers to depart.

Following their departure, Sir Peter stepped forward and shouted "Farewell," but the carriages had rolled along too far down the driveway for anyone to clearly hear him. By the time Samantha looked, she could see Sir Peter sullenly turn toward his mansion, and reenter it with Lady Cornwall.

Chapter 32

The carriages arrived at the Painswick estate by nightfall. After tucking the children into bed upstairs, John grabbed Samantha's hand and led her down to the main floor.

A brief survey of the halls proved what they had hoped—they were alone.

John stood a moment, staring searchingly into Samantha's eyes.

Samantha's love and desire reflected back at him. *I want you so badly, John!*

He pulled her close—gently, but with an unmistakable purpose.

They kissed with all of the intensity that had built up in them during the previous several weeks.

With bodies pressed tightly together, Samantha felt the surging protrusion between John's legs. Her heart throbbed wildly with anticipation. The area between her legs did also, and soon released a flow of moisture.

John ardently spoke. "I have desired this...*you*...for such a long time."

Samantha did not speak. Instead, she guided John to his bedchamber, and closed the door behind them. Once inside, she threw her arms around his neck, and fervently kissed him again. Her tongue moved hungrily inside his mouth, as did his in hers. She pulled his head closer, in an attempt to get inside him as much as possible. "Mmmmmmmm." The sound originated from deep within her throat. *Finally alone together!*

She led him over to his bed, where they sat down. She kissed his neck, his ears, and as she undressed him, his chest, and lower abdomen. She rubbed John's breeches between his legs. A yearning whimper escaped her mouth as she became aware of the handsome size and structure of his manhood. *Amazing! So large and firm!*

Undoing John's breeches, Samantha pulled them down with his assistance. She licked from the base of his manhood to its tip.

Exquisite!

Sitting upright, she unbuttoned the top part of her dress, allowing John full view of her breasts for the first time.

John stared in awe. "Samantha... You are more beautiful than I even imagined."

He tenderly held each breast in his hands, and ran his tongue around each erect nipple.

As his tongue circulated, Samantha moaned softly. "That feels so good," she voiced.

Releasing hold of one of her breasts, John moved his hand underneath her dress, and worked his way upward and underneath her underclothing. Locating the place between her legs now wet with moisture, he worked his middle finger inside her.

"Ahhhhh!" Samantha moaned blissfully.

John moved his finger in and out while holding tight to the area between Samantha's legs.

He thrust his tongue hard into her mouth.

Samantha moaned, "Mmmmmmmmm."

She pulled her mouth away. "I want you in me now!"

John removed his hand, and Samantha hurriedly unbuttoned the rest of her dress. She fully removed her underclothing, and lay back on John's bed exposing her entire nakedness. Her eyes pleaded him to mount her. *I can wait no longer!*

John surveyed Samantha's body, now drenched in moonlight. His eyes followed the path from her sumptuous breasts, along her curving waistline, to the small tuft of hair between her legs.

Tearing off the remainder of his clothing, he climbed on top of her, and looked down into her eyes. His expression conveyed, "Your ever longing desire will soon be fulfilled!"

Samantha's eyes pleaded further. *Please satisfy my aching insides now!*

John spread her legs with one knee, and she spread them farther apart unfolding her entire nether region for his visual pleasure.

He marveled at her glistening wetness.

Lowering his torso, he touched Samantha's entrance with the tip of his regal manhood.

Shivers scintillated up and down her spine, and she moaned her excitement.

John moved forward and back, softly teasing her velvety labia eliciting further anticipation.

"Uhhhhhhhhh!" Samantha moaned; this time almost painfully desirous. Wrapping her arms around John's backside, she drew him close to her tightly.

John lifted his hips, and thrust himself deeply inside her.

Samantha cried out her ecstasy. Her insides burned with pleasure. *Thank God!* "That feels really good, John!"

"*You* feel really good," John reciprocated.

Their eyes seared into each other's; their hips moved up and down.

Samantha grabbed John's buttocks, pulling him deeply inside her. She coaxed, "Harder!"

John complied. He rubbed her insides with long, intense, heated strokes.

Samantha reveled in the sight of John's pleasing hardness as it entered and emerged from her body. *Heaven could be no better than this!*

She vocalized her pleasure from deep in the back of her throat.

The sound of Samantha's enjoyment spurred John's excitement to the level of animalistic agitation.

Her vocalizations increased in intensity; his guttural sounds intensified. Soon, they could restrain themselves no longer. Their climax reached its crescendo; bodies tensing.

John collapsed gently on top of Samantha.

Exhausted but completely satisfied; their nude, entangled bodies relaxed.

A short while later, John lifted his head and gazed down at Samantha.

Her moonlit face only inches away from his; she stared up into her beloved's eyes.

John's lips curved into a slight smile. "I love you, Beautiful."

Samantha smiled. Her heart pounded. "I love *you*, Handsome."

Still wrapped in a loving embrace, John returned his head to a pillow. They closed their eyes, and fell asleep.

Chapter 33

During the afternoon following their return, John's guards watched a messenger pound the following note into a tree outside the main entrance gate:

LEEVE OR DIE!

IVAN

Ivan had obviously arranged for someone to wait for John's return in order to deliver the threatening message.

By the following week, Ivan's band of brutes approached John's estate and boisterously set up camp nearby.

Hearing the bawdy band approach, John equipped his guards with the latest model of Brown Bess .75 caliber flintlock, and lined them several feet in front of the stone wall surrounding his mansion. He, too, held a Brown Bess prepared to fight.

The brutes—carrying axes, hatchets, and cleavers—fearlessly advanced to John's mansion. Arriving at the stone wall, they lined up before John's guards outsizing them by almost twice.

Ivan, the most colossal, stood behind his line laughing erratically.

Before John could give the word to fire, one of the brutes cleaved the head from one of his guards.

"Fire!" John shouted.

Initially, Ivan's band seemed impenetrable. The guards' musket balls ricocheted ineffectively off of them. As the guards fired, the brutes savagely approached hacking at bodies—blood spurting and limbs projecting in all directions.

By pure grit and determination, John's line discharged continual fire.

One by one an injured brute vacated the premises until only Ivan remained.

Ivan and John stared at each other.

All became eerily quiet.

Finally, Ivan spat on the ground and lumbered off. John had triumphed.

"We won!" shouted one of John's guards.

More joined in, "We won the battle!" They looked at John for his approval.

John eyed his bloody battleground, and somberly responded, "We won *this* battle ..."

With that, he turned away, and walked to his mansion.

Inside the mansion, John found Samantha with the children hunkered down on the servant floor. Bloody, filthy, and with a grim expression, he voiced, "Samantha..."

Samantha turned towards him. "John!"

She ran to him, and clutched him tightly. "Thank God you are alive! I feared terribly for you!"

John remained silent.

"What happened?" Samantha asked. "What distresses you? Did Ivan win?"

"No... We won... But, Ivan *also* won."

"What do you mean?" Samantha felt confused.

John clarified, "We drove off Ivan and his beasts. However, my guards took too much punishment. It would have been a consummate victory had we fought on a distant ground. But this is my home...where my loved ones reside..."

Pensively, John turned toward his servants. "The dead and wounded require our attention..."

Facing Samantha again, he inquired, "Will you take the children upstairs and stay with them?"

"Of course."

John nodded his thanks, and returned to the battle site at the front of his mansion.

Chapter 34

A few evenings after the battle, with the dead buried and the wounded returned to their homes, John fell into a deep sleep. He awoke in the predawn hours, and crept quietly into Samantha's bedchamber. "Samantha, wake up."

"John?"

"Yes. Samantha, I feel I have had a presentiment."

Samantha sleepily inquired, "What do you mean?"

"I feel as though I have had a glimpse of our future. I believe if I follow through with a few things, all will fall into place and we will live out our lives happily."

Samantha stretched and sat upright. "Tell me more!"

"In a vivid dream—seemingly more genuine than conjured—I saw us living out our days in the American Colonies..." John grabbed both of her arms. "What do you think of that? Would you consider removing yourself and the children to America?"

"John," Samantha began. "I would go *anywhere,* as long as I could live there with you." She blinked her eyes in an attempt to see more clearly.

"Anywhere?" John asked.

"*Anywhere,* my love!"

"Absolutely?"

"*Absolument!*" Samantha affirmed in French.

John pulled Samantha close, kissing her several times on her neck. "You enchant me, *ma cherie*, when you speak French!"

Samantha happily laughed. Stars shone from her eyes. Reaching out her hands, she positioned John's head to better kiss his mouth. She rose to her knees, and kissed him fervently, pushing her tongue deep inside.

John gently pushed her flat on her back, and climbed on top of her. Kneeling over her, he said, "But, now you must work on your American English!"

Samantha laughed and joked, "I can sing Yankee Doodle!"

John laughed. "How about you bolt the door, and show me!"

"My pleasure!"

John helped Samantha up. She walked to the door, and bolted it. Turning back around, she gazed at him a moment. She unfastened her nightgown, and let it drop to the floor. Completely nude, she seductively inquired, "How about I save the song for another time? "

John approached her. He lifted her, and carried her to the bed where he set her down gently.

She pulled him close; and there, they made passionate love until dawn's light glimmered through the bedchamber window.

Chapter 35

Later that morning, as waking children and servants filled the French Renaissance mansion with happy rustlings, John knocked at Samantha's bedchamber door.

When Samantha answered it, John pretended he had not seen her since the evening before. "Good morrow, Sweetheart! Would you care to take a walk with me?"

"I would love to!" Samantha played along.

They soon met outdoors behind the mansion.

"Lovely day," John commented. "So much warmer than usual for January." He turned to gaze at her a moment as they walked.

"I quite agree...but then I *always* feel warm with *you* in my presence." Samantha glanced at him coquettishly.

John grinned.

A minute or two later, he became serious. "I sent a message to my brother informing him I find it necessary to return with you and the children."

Samantha's expression conveyed "Please continue." Inwardly she thought, *Dear Lord, not there again!*

"I resolve to leave you and the children at Peter's whilst I travel to America to forge a new way of life."

Samantha stopped walking, and faced him. "I believe in you, John. If that is what you desire, I support you fully." *That is how much I love you. I would sacrifice almost anything for the chance of being with you in the end!*

John nodded, and they continued walking. Once they had traveled deep into the woods, he stopped alongside a babbling brook. Facing Samantha, he grabbed both of her arms.

Their eyes blazed ardently.

John knelt down on one knee, and grabbed Samantha's left hand.

Samantha gasped. She knew what this pose signified. Her right hand went to her heart. *Dear Lord! I think he plans to propose!*

Looking up, John earnestly spoke, "My sweet, beautiful Samantha... Before you came into my life, I thought I would live out my days with only emptiness in a large portion of my heart. But during these past several months, that empty place has been filled with a love deeper than I have ever felt before. I fear I could not be happy without you by my side. Therefore, it is my sincerest request..."

Samantha smiled adoringly while John looked down at the ground and cleared his throat.

Returning his eyes to hers, John inquired, "Samantha...will you marry me?"

Samantha pulled on John's hand to signal him to stand.

John rose to his feet, and Samantha looked up into his eyes. She sincerely and emphatically responded, "Yes!"

Reaching into his cloak pocket, John pulled out a silver, marquise-cut diamond ring. He placed it over the tip of Samantha's left ring finger. "This ring belonged to my mother. She was the last person to wear it... I would be honored if you would take it to wear for the rest of your days."

Samantha moved the ring into place on her finger. With tears in her eyes, she vowed, "I will cherish this ring as long as I live." She wrapped her arms around John, and kissed him while tears of happiness ran down her cheeks.

John grabbed Samantha's face with both of his hands. He held her still, and conveyed his thoughts through his eyes.

You melt my heart when you look at me that way! Pure love and happiness! Samantha reached out her right hand, and touched John's face tenderly.

He kissed each tear-covered cheek.

Taking off his cloak, he spread it out on the ground and sat down on it. He reached for her hand, and pulled her gently towards him.

There, alongside the babbling brook, John and Samantha made love for the second time that morning—this time, with Samantha unabashedly *and loudly* voicing her euphoria until the moment John made his final thrust deeply inside her.

Chapter 36

Two days later, one of John's guards sent on reconnaissance spotted Ivan's brutes in a nearby village.

Once informed, John set up Samantha in Painswick's Old Castle Inn, paying the innkeeper an exorbitant sum for his silence. "I am taking the children to Peter's directly," he told Samantha. "I have arranged for you to join them after I leave for the Colonies."

Does this mean he will marry me without the children being present? Samantha looked away from him, while wondering. *Is this elegant chamber where we will celebrate our honeymoon? Or, will he only marry me after he has returned from the American Colonies?*

No...I dare not ask. If I am overeager, it might bring bad luck. He will let me know soon enough. Samantha looked back at John, and nodded her head. Her lips formed a slight smile.

John kissed her briefly. "I will return to you in two to three days."

He exited the inn, and headed for his estate to round up the children.

Chapter 37

The following day, John and the children stood before the Stow-on-the-Wold Gothic mansion.

Sir Peter stepped outside to greet them. He hugged John, and heartily exclaimed, "Come in! Come in!"

As each boy entered, he shook his hand. With each girl, he put on a fancy show of grasping her hand and bowing to kiss it.

After receiving their hand-kiss, Tabitha and Rachel happily giggled and ran to hug Lady Cornwall's legs.

Exhibiting a genuine smile, Lady Cornwall extended her arms. "Welcome back! We missed you!" She brought her arms down around the little girls, and gave them a light squeeze.

"We missed you, too, Lady Cornwall!" voiced Tabitha and Rachel. They briefly curtseyed.

"Escort the children to the banquet hall!" Sir Peter ordered the maidservants standing nearby.

The maidservants followed their instructions with the exception of one maidservant. This maidservant remained behind, and looked questioningly at Lady Cornwall.

"See that they are well-nourished, Priscilla."

"Yes'm...m'Lady Sue." Priscilla bowed her head. She eyed Lady Cornwall amorously, and headed to the kitchen.

Lady Cornwall gazed after her adoringly, and followed.

John caught the exchange, and looked at his brother. Raising an eyebrow, he said, "So!"

Sir Peter's nod conveyed, "Yes, you are correct, and it is perfectly fine by me." He gestured towards the gallery with his right hand. "Shall we?"

John nodded, and they walked inside to sit down at their regular places.

"So tell me your plan." Sir Peter adjusted himself in his seat, and filled his pipe. Looking intently, he said, "Your messenger only afforded me bits and pieces."

"Before summer concludes..." John began, "I shall have made my way to America, set the foundation for my future, and be returned for the others. At that time..." John cleared his throat. "I plan to marry Samantha in a private ceremony—hopefully witnessed by you, Susan, and the children—before setting out for the Colonies as a complete family."

Sir Peter sat silently a long moment. He inhaled and exhaled deeply. "Very well, my dear brother..." he spoke slowly. "I know that once you have set your mind to something, there is no use trying to persuade you otherwise."

"Do I have your support?"

"Yes," Sir Peter fully conceded. "You have my support."

John nodded and grinned.

Sir Peter drew in another deep breath. Looking away from John, he exhaled and closed his eyes. "You shall be missed..." Returning his eyes to his brother, he added, "I pray only for your exceeding happiness and good health."

John nodded and said, "And, I, for you and Susan as well..."

"Where did you say Samantha is?"

239

"She will join you in a few days." John reflected a short moment. Grinning, he said, "She had some unfinished business to attend to in Painswick."

Sir Peter presented a slight smile. He stood up, and shook John's hand. "Come! Let us avail you with some nourishment."

John followed Sir Peter to the banquet hall, where they joined the children for a blissful meal.

Chapter 38

After breakfast the next morning, John and a male servant saddled and packed his horse. Reentering his brother's mansion, he found everyone in the dance hall. He called Adam and Ethan to stand before him. "I am assigning you gentlemen the responsibility of assisting Sir Peter with any manly duty he so requires."

They proudly responded, "Yes, sir!"

John shook their entrusted hands.

Next, he summoned Amanda, Tessa, and Sarah. "You, young ladies, are to assist Lady Cornwall and Mistress Talbot with whatever womanly endeavor they may require."

"Yes, sir!" the girls responded happily.

John bent down to hug them.

Lady Cornwall stepped forward. "Please inform the children..."

John stood up, and waited for her to finish.

Lady Cornwall cleared her throat nervously. "All of the children are welcome to address me as their *Aunt Susan* from this day forth!"

John smiled and winked at Lady Cornwall.

She blushed, and presented an affirming nod.

"You heard your *Aunt Susan*, children!" John spoke heartily. He turned, and exited by the front door of the mansion.

The smaller children ran outside, and gathered around him for their hugs and kisses.

After doling out his affection, John rose to his feet and found Sir Peter standing next to him. Embracing him, he said, "I am forever indebted to you, my dear brother... Farewell."

"Farewell," Sir Peter solemnly responded.

John faced Lady Cornwall. "Farewell, *Aunt Susan!*"

She smiled warmly, and looked shyly toward the ground.

John walked to his horse, and jumped up onto it. He grabbed his hat, and waved it at everyone. "Farewell, loved ones!"

Turning his horse to the direction of Painswick, he spurred it hard.

Chapter 39

    A plenitude of stars shone through a crisp, winter night sky when John entered Samantha's room at the Old Castle Inn. With a loving gleam in his eyes, he announced, "Hello, Beautiful!"

To be continued...